"Each of Mazer's eight stories treats with perception and sensitivity the maturing of a teenage girl."
—(starred review) *ALA Booklist*

"With precision and compassion, Mazer dissects small moments of defiance and self-discovery that subtly alter the lives of each of her heroines."
—(starred review) *School Library Journal*

"Powerful and poignant . . . [Mazer is one of] five of the best of the practitioners writing for young people today."—*The New York Times Book Review*

"Recommended."—(starred review) *Bulletin of the Center for Children's Books*

NORMA FOX MAZER is the author of *Saturday, the Twelfth of October*, called "a well-paced, unusual fantasy" by *ALA Booklist*, and *A Figure of Speech*, a National Book Award finalist, both from Delacorte Press. Ms. Mazer lives in Syracuse, New York, with her husband, novelist Harry Mazer, and the youngest of their four children.

THE LAUREL-LEAF LIBRARY brings together under a single imprint outstanding works of fiction and nonfiction particularly suitable for young adult readers both in and out of the classroom. The series is under the editorship of Charles F. Reasoner, Professor of Elementary Education, New York University.

DEAR BILL, REMEMBER ME?

And Other Stories by
NORMA FOX MAZER

Published by
DELL PUBLISHING CO., INC.
1 Dag Hammarskjold Plaza
New York, New York 10017

Laurel-Leaf Library ® TM 766734, Dell Publishing Co., Inc.

ISBN: 0-440-91749-2

Reprinted by arrangement with Delacorte Press.
Printed in the United States of America
First Laurel-Leaf printing—January 1978
Second Laurel-Leaf printing—June 1978
Third Laurel-Leaf printing—August 1978
Fourth Laurel-Leaf printing—February 1979
Fifth Laurel-Leaf printing—July 1979
Sixth Laurel-Leaf printing—November 1979

For my sisters, Adele and Linda

CONTENTS

Up on Fong Mountain

TO: All Students Taking English 10
MEMO FROM: Carol Durmacher
DATE: February 3

"That favorite subject, Myself." —JAMES BOSWELL

Your term project will be to keep a weekly Journal. Purchase a 7¾ x 5–inch ruled, wire-bound notebook. (Woolworth's at the Mall stocks them, so does Ready's Stationers on East Avenue.) Date each entry. Note the day, also. Make a minimum of two entries each week. The Journal must be kept to the end of the school year. It is to be handed in June 24.

I will not read these Journals—only note that they have been kept faithfully. There will be two marks for this project—Pass and Fail. Only those students not handing in a Journal or blatantly disregarding the few rules I have set down will receive a Fail.

In writing in your Journal, try to be as free as possible. This is *your* Journal: express *yourself*. Use the language that comes naturally to you. Express your true feelings without reservation. Remember, I will not read what you have written (unless you ask me to). Once I record your mark I will hand the Journal back to you. (You may be present while I check to see that the Journal has been kept in the required manner.)

These Journals are for YOU. To introduce you to the joys of record-keeping. To help you think about your lives, the small events, the little graces, the funny, sad, or joyful moments. Record these as simply and directly as possible.

A moment recorded is a moment forever saved.

Carol Durmacher

February 6, Thursday

I don't know what to write really. I have never kept a journal before. Well, I better write something. I have to do this two times in the next three days. Miss Durmacher, you said, Write your true feelings. My true feelings are that I actually have nothing to write. Well, I'll describe myself. My name is Jessie Granatstein. I'm fifteen years old. My coloring is sandy (I think you would call it that). I ought to lose ten pounds. My eyes are brown. I have thick eyebrows that my sister Anita says I ought to pluck. My father says I'm stubborn as a bulldog. He said that last week when we fought over the Sunday papers. I was up first and started to read it, then he got up and took it away from me. He says he ought to get it first, the whole paper, every single section, because he's the father, the head of the household, and that I should learn to wait patiently. We argued for an hour. He didn't change my mind and I didn't change his. He got the paper first.

February 8, Saturday

Anita and I made a *huge* bowl of popcorn tonight, then ate it watching TV. Then we were still hungry, so we made a pot of spaghetti, slathered it with butter, and ate it straight from the pot. We had a good time till Mark came over, then Anita acted like I didn't exist.

February 12, Wednesday

Lincoln's birthday, also my parents' anniversary. Mom made a rib roast, baked Idaho potatoes with sour cream and chives, frozen corn on the cob, and strawberry short-cake with real whipped cream for topping. I stuffed myself like a pig. It half rained, half snowed all day. Why would anyone want to get married on Feb. 12, in the middle of winter? Mom just laughs when I ask her, and looks at Dad. "Sex rears its ugly head," I whispered to Anita. "Don't be vulgar," she said.

3

February 14, Friday

I don't have anything to write. I'm sorry, Miss Durmacher, but all I seem to be writing about is food. I had tuna fish with celery and mayo for lunch, plus two ice cream sandwiches which I should have resisted. Mom says not to worry about my weight, that I'm "appealing." She's nice.

February 18, Tuesday

Yesterday I was talking to Anita and we got called to supper right in the middle of a sentence. "Girls!" That's my father, he won't eat till we're all at the table, and he's hungry when he sits down, so he doesn't want to wait very long for us. Like, not one extra second.

But, anyway, that wasn't what I was going to write about today. I was going to write about Brian Marchant —Brian Douglas Marchant III. Kids call him BD. I'm pretty sure he was watching me in geometry class today. Fairly sure, although not positive. What I am positive of is that *I* was watching *him*. In fact—well, I'm not going to write any more about it. I thought I wanted to, but I take it back. And that's all I have to say today.

Feb. 21, Fri.

Well, Miss D., it's a Friday, it's winter, I feel sort of depressed. I wish I had someone I could really talk to.

4

It snowed again today. I've always loved snow, loved to see it caked in big thick white clumps on all the trees when it first falls, loved to jump around in it. Today, for the first time ever I didn't like it. I *hated* it. And that depressed me even more.

And to tell the truth, Miss D., while we're on depressing subjects, I just can't believe this journal. Almost three more *months* of my real thoughts and feelings—that's depressing!

Monday, February 24

Brian Marchant borrowed paper from me, and winked at me. I have always hated winking boys.

Feb 28, last day of the month, Friday

BD winked at me again.

I said, "Why are you winking at me?"

"What do you mean? I'm winking at you because I feel like winking at you."

"Don't," I said.

"Don't?" He looked at me in astonishment and amazement. I mean it, Miss Durmacher, like nobody ever said don't to him before.

"I think winking is dumb," I said.

He stared at me some more. Then he gave me a double wink.

5

March 3, Monday

I saw BD in the cafeteria today. I said, Hi. He said, Hi. I said, Have you given up winking? He said, What? Then he laughed. He has a nice big laugh.

Tues. Mar. 4

BD and I ate lunch together today. No winking.

Thursday, March 6

Lunch again with BD. I forgot to bring mine and didn't have any money with me, either. BD brings *enormous* lunches. Two peanut butter jelly sandwiches, one tuna fish with pickle relish, one salami with cheese, three Hostess Twinkies, one bag of chips, an apple, an orange, a banana, plus he bought three cartons of milk and two ice cream sandwiches. And parted reluctantly with one of the pbj's for me. Also, he bigheartedly gave me half his apple.

And that makes *three* entries for this week, Miss Durmacher. Not bad, huh?

Tuesday, March 11

BD walked home with me and came in for cocoa. Then we went outside and he looked up at the pignut tree in the backyard which is almost the tallest tree around. "I think I could climb that, Jess," he said.

"Don't, BD," I said.

"Why not? I like to climb trees."

"I don't like heights, and it might be slippery."

"You don't have to climb it," he said. And up he went. I could hardly bear to look. All I could think was, He's going to fall. He's going to fall and crack his head.

When he got nearly to the top he yelled, "Jess-eee! Jess-eee!" I yelled back, "I hear you, Beee-Deee!" Then he came down, laughing all the way.

Wednesday, March 12

Anita said she thought BD was funny-looking. I said I didn't think he was any funnier-looking than most human beings.

She said, "You have to admit he's, one, shorter than you, and two, has got big pop eyes. Green pop eyes, like a frog. Also, a big mouth which looks like he could swallow your whole face when he kisses you."

"How do you know he kisses me, Anita?"

"Well, sister, I hope he kisses you! At your age, you're not going to tell me you're sweet fifteen and never been kissed! I had boys running after me and kissing me since I was nine years old!" She laughed merrily.

Are you reading this, Miss Durmacher? Don't, please. The truth is, I have only been kissed a few times—well, not even a few, three to be exact—at parties. But I'm not going to tell Anita that.

March 21, Friday

Anita doesn't stop making cracks about BD's looks. I just don't understand it. Her boyfriend, Mark Maloff, is supposed to be super-good-looking, but I really can't stand him. He wears pink ties and has a little green ring on his left hand. It's true BD looks as if he never thinks about what he's wearing. Nothing ever matches. But something about him really pleases me. Maybe it's the way he walks around with his hands stuck in his back pockets, sort of jaunty and jolly and swaggering. (The other day he was wearing one green sock and one dark blue. When I pointed it out to him, he said, "Really?" and looked down at his feet, very interested. Then he said that his eyes were never really open in the morning, not till about ten o'clock, and by then, for better or worse, he was dressed.)

Saturday night, March 22

Miss Durmacher, don't read this—you said you wouldn't. I love kissing BD. I love it!

Wednesday, March 26

Mom thinks she and I are alike. She's always saying it. (She thinks Dad and Anita are alike, she says they are both very good-looking. True. While she and I are both chunky and sandy-haired.) *But* Mom doesn't say boo to Dad, she's always very sweet to him. (Actually she's sort of sweet to everybody.) I'm not like her in that way *at all*. *I'm not sweet*. In that regard, I'm more like my father than Anita is. I became aware of this because of BD. I have been noticing that he likes things his own way. Most of the time he gets it. I have noticed, too, that I don't feel sweet about this at all!

March 29, Sat. afternoon

BD came over last night and said we were going bowling. I said why didn't we do something else, as we went bowling last week. He said he liked bowling and what else was there to do, anyway? I said we could go roller skating. BD laughed a lot. I said what's the problem with roller skating. I like roller skating. (Which I do.) BD said, "Jessie, why are you being so picky? Why are you being hard to get along with?" I thought, Right! Why am I?

And we went bowling. And then, later, I realized, just like that, he had talked me out of what I wanted to do and into what he wanted to do.

Monday, March 31, last day of the month

I don't even mind writing in here anymore, Miss Durmacher. I have plenty to write all the time. Now, lately, I've been thinking about what you wrote at the top of our assignment sheet. That favorite subject, Myself. Everyone got a laugh out of that when we first read it. Who wants to admit they are their own best, most favorite topic of conversation?

But I think it's the truth. Last night, at supper, Dad was talking, and I noticed how I was pretty much waiting to get my own two cents in. It seems Anita was, too, because she actually beat me to the punch. The only one who didn't rush to talk about herself was Mom, and sometimes I think that's just from long years of practice listening to Dad.

Also, today, I noticed when BD and I were hanging around school that he is another one whose most favorite subject is—myself. That is—*himself*. The thing is, I really like to listen to him go on because, mainly, I like him. But if he never wants to listen to me, after a while, I get this horrible lonely feeling. I think that's it. A lonely feeling. Sad.

April 2, Tuesday, no I mean, Wednesday

A dumb fight with BD today. He came home from school with me and not for the first time got going on his ancestors who came over here about 200 years ago. *Pioneers*, he said with a big happy delighted smile. As if because they got on a boat about 150 years earlier than my family this made them really special. So I said, "Well, BD, I think there's another word for your ancestors. Thieves."

"Thieves!" His cheeks puffed up.

"They stole Indian land, didn't they?" (I have just become aware of this lately from Mr. Happy's American History class.)

BD whipped out his map of the Northeast from his

pocket and stabbed his finger about a dozen places all over Maine and Vermont. "Here's Marchantville, Jessie. Marchant River. Marchant's Corners. East Marchant! West Marchant, and Marchant's Falls!" He looked at me very triumphantly.

"BD," I said, "I've seen all that before." Which, indeed, I have. In fact, the first time I realized BD actually carried that map around with him, I burst out laughing. And at the time he didn't take too kindly to that. But this time, I made him truly furious.

"You think thieves were the founders of all these places, Jessie? You think that's why all these rivers and towns were named after the Marchants? They were pioneers, Jess—" And he got that fanatical happy look on his face again at the mere sound of the word. "Pioneers, people who had the intelligence and foresight to go to the new country, the unexplored territory, the virgin lands—"

"Now listen, BD," I said, and I had to talk loud to slow him down. "Suppose a boatload of people came over here tomorrow from China and landed smack in the middle of our town, and pushed us all out—"

"The boat's in the middle of our town?" BD said.

"You know what I mean! The people, BD. The people from across the ocean. And they say to us, From now on, we're going to call this Fong City after our leader, Mao Tze Fong, and this river here, this is going to be Fong River, and over here we've got Fong Mountain—"

"Jessie, that's dumb," BD yelled. "That's inaccurate, the comparison just won't work—"

Well! I can yell, too. *"Like I was saying*, BD, although

11

we don't know it, the Chinese have developed this ray gun. Instant death. Superior to anything we have. Okay? Now—"

"No, it's not okay. We've got atomic weapons, we've got sophisticated weapons, an army, police—"

"So here comes Mao Tze Fong," I went on, "and all the others with him and they've got these ray guns which we can't do *anything* against. They kill off a bunch of us, take over our houses and land, and the rest of us run to hide in the mountains—"

"Fong Mountain, I presume?" BD said.

"Right! We're up on Fong Mountain. From there we survivors would try to get our homes back, but after quite a few years of battling, the invaders would beat us enough so we'd have to agree to anything they said. Because, remember, we have just a few old hunting rifles against their ray guns. They, after a while, would let us have some land they didn't care about, some swamps and stuff, and they'd stick us all on it and call it a reservation. And meanwhile, *meanwhile*—BD, are you listening?—they'd have been wiping out all the old maps and making new ones. With Fong Mountain, East Fong, West Fong, Fong's Corners, and *fongoo*, BD, if you don't want to understand the point of what I'm saying!"

April 3, Thursday

In geometry class today: "How's your revered ancestors, BD?"

"How're things up on Fong Mountain, Jessie?"

April 6, Sunday

I talked to BD on the phone. We were peaceful. That's good. Because we have been fighting a good bit lately.

April 12, Saturday

Mom came into my room with a sweater she'd washed for me. "Oh, by the way, honey," she said (which is always the signal that she's going to be serious), "aren't you and Brian seeing an awful lot of each other?"

"Me and BD?" I said, sort of stalling for time.

"Yes. You saw him every single night this week. Do you think that's wise?"

"Wise?"

"I don't want you to be in a terrible hurry like I was."

"Terrible hurry?"

"To grow up," she said.

"Grow up?"

"Jessie! Do you have to repeat everything I say?" She flashed me a funny little smile. "When two people see a lot of each other, it's not always so wise. They might get too—they might get carried away."

"Oh," I said. "You don't have to worry, Mom. No one is going to carry me away."

Tuesday, April 15

Thinking about me and BD. At this point in my life, the way I feel is—my body is my body. And I don't care

13

to share it with anyone. I don't know totally why I feel that way, and I don't think I have to know why. It's just the way I feel. Sometimes in the morning I look at myself in the mirror and I feel proud. I look myself all over and I think, Hey, yeah, Jessie, that's your body. Terrific!

Sunday, April 20

A fight with BD last night. Please don't read this, Miss Durmacher! It's private and personal. We were parked in the cemetery. BD said I was being mean. He said I was being selfish, and also unfair. I didn't know what to say in return, so I just got mad. I said, I'm going home! I wanted to get out of the car and walk but he wouldn't let me. He started the car and drove me home. I was furious. He won't even let me get mad in my own way.

Monday, April 21

Miss Durmacher, you didn't say how long or short the entries had to be. I'll describe the weather today. Sletty gray air and the smell of garbage everywhere.

Tuesday, April 22

Today, in school, I saw BD in the halls, and I saw him in geometry class, and I saw him in the cafeteria. We looked at each other. He didn't say anything, and I didn't say anything.

After school I started home. After a few blocks I felt someone was following me. I turned around. There was BD behind me. I started walking again. Then I turned around. He was right behind me. He grabbed me in a big hug, knocking my books every which way and said, "Kiss! Kiss!" I was sort of shocked, but I couldn't help kissing him back. And then he laughed and laughed.

Wednesday, April 30

Today I tried to talk to BD. He says it's my fault we fight so much. He says I pick the fights, that I'm aggressive, he's peaceful. This might be true. He is peaceful when he gets his way. He said I didn't know how to give in gracefully. He might be right about this, too. I hate to lose a game or an argument. He says I'm a prickly character. He's started calling me Porky, short for porcupine.

Sunday, May 4

Last night BD and I parked down by the river. Cars were lined up for a mile, all of them dark, all of them looking empty. Ha-ha. I told BD I felt like I'm part of a factory production make-out line. BD just laughed. He always laughs when he doesn't want to answer. Anyway, he was getting down to business. He's been doing that lately—and we've been fighting about it. A standoff, so far.

"BD, let's kiss," I said. I really like kissing that boy.

"Sure," he said, but he didn't stop what he was doing.

So I said, "Quit that, BD, you're getting friendlier than I want you to be."

"Oh, don't you like that?" he said, sort of sweet and surprised. "It feels nice. You are so nice and soft, Jessie. I bet your sister and Mark do this—"

I gave him a little shove. "What's it to you what Anita and Mark do? That sounds sick to me."

"Porky," he said.

"Don't call me Porky," I said. "I don't like it."

"Seems like there are a lot of things you don't like, Jessie," he said. "Don't you trust me?"

"I don't see what that's got to do with anything, BD," I said. "But come to think of it—if I gave you $100 to keep for me, I guess you wouldn't spend it, but what if I gave you one thousand?"

"Jessie, that's silly, you don't have a thousand dollars."

"Answer the question, BD," I said. "If I gave you one thousand dollars to keep for me, and then I went away, would you spend my thousand dollars?"

"No, I wouldn't, Jessie. I wouldn't spend one single *penny* of your money."

"What if I gave you that thousand dollars and then I didn't come back for ten years? What if you were told, by someone you knew was trustable, that I was dead. Would you spend my money?"

"Jessie, is this going to be another Fong Mountain," BD said. "Let's get back to the subject. I said you could trust me, and I meant it. I'll be careful."

"Careful. What does that mean?"

"Well, you know, I won't, uh, hurt you—"

16

"Hurt me?"

"Well, you know, maybe you're afraid of—"

"I'm not afraid, BD."

"If you're not afraid, then why won't you—?"

"Not being afraid isn't a reason to do something. Just because you're not afraid of heights doesn't mean you're going to take a walk along the edge of the Empire State Building."

"I'm not talking about the Empire State Building, Jessie," he said in this patient voice.

"I know what you're talking about, BD," I said, and suddenly I had the feeling that I was up there on Fong Mountain again. And I was all alone. And I thought, Oh! I wish I had someone to talk to.

Saturday, May 10

I have kind of a problem here. What I want to write about is BD and me, but I keep thinking you'll read this, Miss Durmacher. Your eyes might just slip and catch this or that. And if they do, you're going to just keep reading. That's human nature. So this is going to be my second entry for the week.

Friday, May 16

Oh, BD, you mix me up . . . I love you . . . but . . .

Friday, May 23

BD came over last night. I thought we could just walk around, buy ice cream, and maybe talk. Be restful with each other. It was a nice night, warm, and I didn't feel like doing anything special. Also, BD couldn't get the car, which was a relief to me because we wouldn't have to park and then fight over me.

But the minute we set foot on the sidewalk, BD said, "We're going to the movies," and he starts walking fast, getting ahead of me, like he wanted me to have to run to catch up with him.

So I just kept walking along at my usual pace, and I said to his back, "How do you know that's what I want to do?"

"There's a new movie at the Cinema," he said. "You'll like it."

"How do you know that?"

He turned around, gave me one of his smiles. He really has the nicest smile in the world! But he uses it unfairly. "Oh, listen, Jessie, if I like it, you'll like it. Right?"

"Wrong!" I yelled.

"Say it again, Porky. They couldn't hear you in Rochester."

"Very funny, BD. And I told you not to call me Porky!"

"Why don't you smile more? When you frown like that it makes you look like a teacher."

"What's wrong with teachers?" I said.

"Who said anything was wrong with teachers. Don't change the subject, Jessie."

"BD, you said if I frowned that made me look like a teacher. You meant ugly!"

"I didn't mean anything of the sort," he said. "I was just talking, just using a metaphor."

I knew he thought he had me there, but Miss Durmacher you had just reviewed all this stuff. "You mean a simile," I said. "The moon *is* a balloon is a metaphor. The moon *looks like* a balloon is a simile."

"Don't act smartass! Come on, walk faster, or we'll miss the opening of the movie."

"What movie?"

"The movie we're going to see." BD wasn't smiling now. Neither was I.

"I don't believe I'm going to any movie," I said. "I haven't made up my mind what I want to do tonight. Nobody asked me what I wanted to do, only told me what they wanted to do."

"They," BD said. "There's only one of me."

"Oh, BD," I said, "no, you're a whole government. You're a president, vice-president, and secretary of defense all rolled into one."

"What are you talking about?"

"You know what I'm talking about, BD. How you always have to be Top Banana. The Big Cheese. Always telling me. You're a regular Mao Tze Fong! We're going to do this, we're going to do that, we're going here, we're eating this—don't you think I have a mind of my own? You want your own way all the time. You never ask me anything. You just barrel on ahead. You want to lead me around by the nose!"

"You're being difficult tonight," he said. He was smiling. Only not his usual, regular beautiful smile, more of a toothy mean smile, as if he would like to really bite off my arm instead of talking to me. "You've been difficult just about every time we see each other lately. Now, do you want to see that movie, or don't you?"

"I don't care about the movie," I said. "What I care about is that I have a mind of my own, I am a free person also, and I don't want to be in any dictatorship relationship!"

"Dictatorship relationship," he said. And he laughed. Hee-hee-hee. "You mean a dictatorial relationship. Dictatorial, not dictatorship."

I stared at him. Then I turned around and walked in the other direction. And he didn't come after me, and I didn't go back after him.

Wednesday, May 28

I guess everything really is over with BD and me. We really have broken up. I never would have thought it— breaking up over grammar, not sex.

June 2, Monday

I know I missed making a couple of entries, Miss Durmacher, but I was sort of upset. I'll make some extra ones to make up for it. Anita has a job after school at the telephone company. Mom has been going over every day to help Aunt Peggy, who just had her fifth baby. I don't have anything to do except hang around the house, feeling crummy.

Monday, June 16

I have to wear a horrible uniform, orange with white trim (Mrs. Richmondi is big on orange—all the cups are orange, also the napkins), but other than that, I really like my job. Mrs. Richmondi is nice, too, but she *hates* bare feet. She's got a sign on the door: NO BARE FEET.

Wednesday, June 18

I see BD every day in school and we never say a word, just look at each other and then keep walking.

Mom came in to Dippin DoNuts today and ordered coffee and a jelly doughnut. Then a bunch of kids came pouring in yelling orders, and before I'd really taken in who was there, I thought—BD's here! And my hands got sweaty.

Thursday, June 19

BD came into the doughnut shop today.

It was 6:30. At first I almost didn't recognize him. He was wearing a funny-looking hat that was too big for him, a gray, crumpled fedora with a wide brim like something out of a thirties gangster movie. And a red wool shirt and enormous, huge red-and-white sneakers. And he was smoking a cigarette, had it dragging from his lower lip like Humphrey Bogart or Jimmy Cagney in one of those old-time movies.

23

He sat down at the counter. I wiped my hands down the sides of my uniform. "Yes?" I said, just like I did to anyone who came in. "Can I help you?"

"Cupacawfee," he said, with the cigarette dangling from his mouth.

I poured coffee into the orange mug and set it in front of him. "Would you like a doughnut with your coffee?" I said, which is the next thing I always say to regular customers.

"Yup," he said.

I was nervous. Some of the coffee spilled. I wiped it up. "Cinnamon, plain, sugar, jelly, chocolate, banana, peach, orange, cream, or cinnamon-chocolate?"

"What kind would you recommend?"

"Whatever you like."

"What do *you* think is the best?"

"That depends on your taste," I said.

"Well, what is your taste? What is your favorite?"

"The cinnamon-chocolate."

"Then that's what I'll have," BD said. "Cinnamon-chocolate."

"I thought you didn't like chocolate, BD," I said, putting the doughnut down in front of him.

"Everyone needs an open mind in this world," he said. "I haven't eaten chocolate in quite a few years, so I might just as well try it again, don't you agree, Jessie?"

I stared at him. I wanted to say, BD, is that you?

I went into the kitchen and took a tray of fresh jelly doughnuts back into the shop. With a piece of waxed paper I began arranging them on the shelf.

"You like working here?" BD said to my back.

"Yes."

"I heard from some of the kids you were working here."

"Oh."

"What do you like best about it?"

"The people," I said. I finished arranging the doughnuts.

"You eat a lot of doughnuts?" he said.

I nodded. "Too many."

"I wouldn't mind working in a doughnut shop. They'd lose money on me."

I nodded. I had missed BD an awful lot. I had thought about him nearly every single day. Sometimes I had loved him so much in my thoughts, in my mind, that I could hardly stand it. Sometimes I had hated him just as hard. Now here he was, not more than two feet from me, and all we were talking about was doughnuts.

The door opened and a woman and two little boys came in and sat down. I wiped the counter in front of them. "One coffee, and two hot chocolates," the woman said. "And—let's see, oh, let's splurge, three jelly doughnuts." She smiled at me. The little boys were twirling on the stools.

I took care of them. BD was brushing up the last crumbs of his doughnut and eating them. "Anything else?" I said. His cigarette was smoking on the edge of the ashtray I'd put down next to him. "More coffee?" BD nodded. I could feel him watching me as I got the Silex and poured his coffee. I took a creamer out of the refrigerator under the counter and put it next to his cup.

The woman and two boys finished and she paid. She left me a dime tip on the counter. I put it into my apron pocket and wiped up everything.

"This smoke bothering you?" BD pointed to the cigarette.

"Some," I said.

BD dropped the cigarette on the floor and stepped on it, ground it out beneath his foot like it was his worst enemy he was grinding down to shreds.

"Thank you," I said.

"Cooperation, ma'am," he said, putting on a Western accent. "We strive to co-op-er-ate. For instance, how do you like my hat?"

"Your hat?"

He took off the hat, twirling it on his fingers. "My hat. This venerable, antique, genuine gangster hat. You don't like it, do you?"

"Well—"

"No, I can tell, you don't have to say anything, you think it's an ancient, grungy piece of junk. Okay, Jessie, if that's what you think, then I don't want to wear this hat," BD said. And he opened the door and flipped the hat through. I could see it sailing out into the parking lot. "That's what I mean by cooperation, Jessie."

"You dope, BD," I said. "I liked that hat all right, it's your sneakers I'm not so wild about."

"My sneakers? These genuine red-and-white Converse All-Americans? Jessie! That's all you have to say." He kicked off his sneakers one after the other, and sent them sailing through the door into the parking lot where they joined his hat.

"You're crazy, BD," I said. "You're really impossible."

And just then my boss, Mrs. Richmondi, parked her car outside in the lot. I looked down at BD's bare feet and then at the sign Mrs. Richmondi had tacked on the door. NO BARE FEET.

"BD, here comes my boss," I said, sort of fast. "You better leave." I put his bill on the counter. "Eighty-one cents." My voice was froggy. I felt kind of sick. Because BD and I hadn't said anything real.

BD reached in one pocket, then in another pocket, then into both back pockets. His forehead got red. He reached into his shirt pockets. "I don't have any money," he said.

Mrs. Richmondi was opening the trunk of her car and taking out packages.

"I don't have any money!" he said again. "I must have come out without my wallet." He turned out his pockets, piling a bunch of stuff on the counter. Movie ticket stubs, keys, his map, a pair of sunglasses.

I pushed his stuff toward him. "Put it away," I said. "My boss hates bare feet. BD, you better just *go*. I'll pay for you."

"You will?"

"Yes!" I took eighty-one cents out of my apron pocket and put it in the cash register.

"I'll bring you back the money," he said. "I'll go right home and get it and bring it back."

Mrs. Richmondi was coming to the door now.

"BD, you don't have to do that."

"But, Jessie—"

"BD, she's coming!"

Mrs. Richmondi pushed open the door with her shoulder. And the first thing she saw was BD's feet. "Young man! You have bare feet. You shouldn't have let him in, Jessie. I've told you, no bare feet!" She dropped her packages on the counter with a thud.

"I didn't come in with bare feet," BD said.

Mrs. Richmondi glared at him. "Out!" She pointed to the door.

"I'm going," BD said, "but don't blame—"

"Out!"

BD left. I watched him through the window, cutting across the parking lot. Mrs. Richmondi was talking to me.

"I'm sorry, Mrs. Richmondi," I said. "Excuse me, please." I bolted through the door, snatched up BD's sneakers and hat, and ran after him. "BD! BD!" I thrust the sneakers into his hand and clapped the hat on his head. "Perfectly good sneakers, BD," I said, which wasn't what I wanted to say, at all.

"If you don't like 'em, Jessie, I don't want 'em."

Oh, BD, I thought. Oh, BD! I knew I had to go back in the shop. Mrs. Richmondi was watching us through the window. But we still hadn't said *anything*. Neither of us. And we were just standing there, looking at each other.

"BD," I said. "BD, do you want to be friends?"

"That's what I mean," he said. And then he gave me

a smile, that terrific smile which I'd missed all this time. "That's what I really mean, Jessie."

Friday, June 20

Today I hand in my journal.

When I started writing it way back in February, I didn't even know BD. It's funny. Odd, I mean. So much has happened. And now, this is the last time I'm writing here. I'm not going to do it anymore. I don't care about the past that much. Not when there's tomorrow to think about and look forward to! So, Miss Durmacher, this is it. Please remember your promise not to read this journal. I trust you, Miss Durmacher.

Pass
Carol Durmacher

Peter in the Park

On a clear Monday afternoon in June, Zoe, wearing her blue nylon knapsack, is walking home from school through Walton Park. Which she is not supposed to be doing. Walton Park is forbidden territory. For years she's been told, Walton Park? Alone? Not on your life! Dangerous! Terrible! You don't go there without Marcia, or Mama, or Weezy.

Adjusting her glasses, Zoe looks quickly to either side. Walton Park is notorious. At least twice a year, there's a mugging, a rape, an assault. Zoe shifts her knapsack more comfortably on her shoulders, whistles bravely.

She enters the forbidden land between the two stone gates, follows the narrow winding path through the little pine woods, and past the ragtag rose garden. Now she climbs the hill toward the water tower. So far, she hasn't met one single soul, not one mugger, rapist, or robber. Then she sees a little battered green station wagon parked by the lightning-struck pine. And sitting on the opened tailgate is a skinny, red-bearded guy, his feet extended, his hands behind his head.

He looks dangerous. His face is narrow. *Criminal cast*, Zoe thinks, trying to collect her startled senses. She tenses, ready to run for her life, back the way she's come. But she'll never make it. He'll overtake her. She's underweight, subject to colds, allergies, and asthmatic attacks. Right now, she can feel a thickening in her lungs as Redbeard looks up, sees her.

"Hey!"

Zoe's heart races like a rabbit. Perspiration breaks out all over her face.

"What's the poop on park regulations? They going to let me stay here?"

"I don't know," Zoe gasps, then hurries on, a tightness beneath her ribs. Is he coming after her? Lord! Should she run, or will that just excite him more? She walks as fast as she dares. At the bend in the path she glances over her shoulder. He's still sitting on the tailgate, slumped, indifferent, not even looking at her.

Well, he might have been a mugger. Or a rapist. Lord knows what! Zoe walks past the neglected tennis courts, then the empty blue swimming pool, and finally—safely —out onto Court Place. She continues home in a fine, fine mood. She has walked alone through Walton Park. And here she is, still in one piece. Even after being accosted in the park. *I was accosted in the park by a bearded man. Lord, it was terrifying!* Even if it wasn't totally true, even if she couldn't tell anyone about it, it was something different, anyway. Something unexpected, for a change! She was just an open book to everyone. It was disgusting.

She'd heard Marcia say it before, and hears her say it again that very night, thinking Zoe is asleep. "I tell you," Marcia says, her voice rich with satisfaction, "I know that child like an open book." And Mama and Weezy murmuring in counterpoint. Agreeing. We know that child like an open book.

No, Marcia, you don't! And you, Weezy, and you, Mama, you don't, either. You haven't read every one of my pages. Damn it, no!

The next day Zoe turns off on Walton Avenue, enters the dangerous territory again. She feels wicked, uneasy. Yesterday she was lucky. She got away with it. But today? You did it once, she argues with herself. Okay? But, no, it's not okay. Once is not enough. Once is just a beginning. Here she is, nearly fourteen, in full possession of her senses, ready to enter high school in the fall, and still forbidden to go where she pleases. How can she live with that and respect herself? She can't.

She passes through the little pine woods. Somebody else is in the park today. Two somebody elses. A pair of lovers, only their feet to be seen, sticking out from beneath a bush. She's wearing red sandals, he's wearing blue sneakers. Zoe stares, curious, then tells herself, *That's rude*, looks away, hums under her breath. "Lover, come back to me." One of the songs Mama sings. Mama knows only the first line of *dozens* of songs. Mama sings, *Lover, come back to meee, Lover come back to meeee,* in her light fine voice. And while she's singing, there's an expression on her face Zoe has never fathomed.

She approaches the water tower, then falters. The little green station wagon is in the same place. So is Redbeard. He raises a hand in greeting as if they're old friends. "Hiya!"

"Hi, yourself," Zoe says bravely.

Slight, narrow-faced, Redbeard wears a little gold cross on a chain around his neck, a green tee shirt and baggy khaki pants held up by a piece of twine. "Well, they're letting me stay," he says, "or anyway, nobody's bothered me so far."

"That's good." Zoe walks slowly by him.

"I really dig this old tree," he says. "Must have been hit by lightning, huh?"

"I guess so," she says, stopping. And then, braver still, keeps the conversation going. "We have some fierce lightning storms around here."

"They don't bother me. I just climb into the Fallen Arch and settle down, snug as a bug." He pats the open tailgate.

"The Fallen Arch?" Zoe repeats. "That's cute!"

He laughs. "So are you. Hey, don't run away. I'm Peter Denham. What's your name?"

"Zoe Eberhardt."

"Hey, Zoe—" He reaches over, twitches one of her long blond braids. "I'm going to call you Goldie, okay?"

"Okay," she says softly. She hitches up her knapsack, not sure about all this, talking to this strange fellow. If Marcia knew, oh wow, she'd go up in smoke for sure.

Well, she'll only stay for another minute. Then she has to go home like the wind.

"This is the first time I've been in Syracuse," Peter says. "The salt city. I read up on these things. I've got a master plan to travel all over the United States, see all our cities, learn about them, sniff their air, try out their parks, meet their citizens."

Zoe listens, fascinated. The thing about Peter, she learns, is that he's nineteen and independent. He's making it in the world all by himself. He lives in the Fallen Arch. There's a mattress and sleeping bag in there, a tin box for his clothes, a tiny one-burner propane stove (in case he doesn't have a fireplace where he parks), a small red Coca-Cola cooler, and another box for his books and notebooks and sketchbooks.

Zoe tries to imagine traveling alone through the world, sleeping in a different place every night, no one around in the morning when you wake up. "What about your family?"

He tells her about his mother who's an RN and works nights. "She's okay," he says emphatically. And his two redheaded sisters, Pam and Heather. And then about his father, a Latin teacher. "Sometimes he thinks he's Caesar. You know? I came, I saw, I conquered. Only not *me*," Peter says, poking himself in the chest. "I go my own way."

"I go my own way," Zoe repeats to herself a little later as she runs home. If she's lucky, Marcia won't notice that she's just a little bit late. She *is* lucky. Marcia is outside, working in the garden. Their house has a long narrow yard which, over the years, Marcia has transformed into a miracle of flowers, shrubs, vines, and vegetables. She's squatting among her plants, a cigarette dangling from her lower lip.

"We're going to be swimming in squash and tomatoes this summer, Ducky," she says proudly to Zoe. "Aren't these little tomatoes gorgeous?" Marcia has raised the tomatoes from seed in an aquarium in her bedroom window. She stands up, brushes her knees, hugs Zoe. "How was your day? Give me a kiss, Ducky."

Zoe nuzzles Marcia's cheek. This year Zoe has grown three inches, so they're both the same height, but Zoe is still growing. "Marcia, I think I'm getting taller than you. I think I'm just a little bit taller now," she says, straightening.

"Oooh, it's happened! I knew it was going to happen and now it has. You're right, you little devil, you've grown past me. Well, your mama did it, and Weezy did it, and now you. First my daughters, and now my granddaughter. You're all leaving Marcia behind. You're all going to look down on Marcia." She laughs delightedly, a brisk barking laugh that says she knows darn well no one could ever look down on her or leave her behind, nohow.

No one Zoe knows has a grandmother like Marcia. No one has an aunt like Weezy, with her silk scarves, gold and silver hoops in her ears and on her arms, and little wool berets perched rakishly on her head. No one lives the way she does with mother, grandmother, aunt, and not a father, uncle, or brother in sight. Way back in kindergarten, the kids said, "You ain't got a daddy? Why don't you have a daddy?"

"I got Weezy, I got Mama, I got Marcia," Zoe used to chant. She never missed a daddy, although, off and on, she had been curious about him. Mama always answered her questions. And now and then, her father, Richie Eberhardt, youthful, smiling, mustached, buzzed through her mind on his Harley Davidson with the silver handles, calling *Hiya Zoe honey, sorry about that, I never did like kids very much.*

Richie Eberhardt, she sometimes says to herself, trying to make him real, but he is no more real than Franklyn Birk, who had been her grandfather. Or Bernie Goodmill, Weezy's ex-husband whom she'd married when she was seventeen and left when she was nineteen.

Over the years Zoe has shared a bedroom with first one, then another of the three women. And in each bedroom she has soaked in their stories. Mama's calm statements of fact about Richie Eberhardt. Weezy's tales of misery about Bernie Goodmill. And Marcia's long anecdotes about Franklyn, Zoe's crazy grandfather, who conducted concerts in the middle of the night on Bailey Road wearing only a pair of ski socks.

A little later Mama and Weezy both come home from work. Through the window, Zoe watches Mama getting out of her car. Mama, so tall and straight, fine gold hair held at one side with a tortoiseshell barrette, and those fantastic violet eyes.

The house fills with the delicious smells of Marcia's cooking, Mama's perfume, and with the sound of Weezy's hoarse laugh. She turns on the radio for music, Mama runs her shower.

"Soup's on," Marcia calls, and they all gather at the round oak dining-room table. "I've been thinking," Zoe says, about the time dessert is being served, "what's wrong with Walton Park? It's pretty, a nice place to walk, and a shortcut for me—"

Mama's violet eyes open wider. "Oh, no, we've talked about that—"

"That's a stupid idea, Ducky," Marcia says with finality.

"I'm not stupid."

"Of course you're not stoo-pid," Weezy agrees. "Mama didn't mean that, Zoey. Anyway, I'm the one who's stoo-pid, not you!" Weezy's talked Zoe out of plenty of things with a laugh and a joke. But still . . .

"Why can't I walk through the park if I feel like it? That's a simple question. Can I please have a simple answer."

"Oooh, oh! Rebellion in the ranks," Weezy teases.

"I'm almost fourteen," Zoe persists. "I *am* fourteen. This Saturday is my birthday."

"Almost forgot," Weezy says with an elaborate wink.

"Just the point," Marcia says, blowing smoke through her nose like a gray-haired dragon. "Just the point, Ducky. That's your simple answer—you're only fourteen years old."

And on that, all three of them—Mama, Weezy, Marcia—agree. Being fourteen is just as dangerous as being four.

"Fourteen and fifteen are the ages," Mama says.

"Sixteen," Weezy puts in. "Defi-*nute*ly, sixteen."

"Fourteen, fifteen, sixteen," Marcia says. "We've got our eyes on you, Ducky." And they all laugh. Zoe laughs, also. How can she not laugh with those three pairs of friendly, loving eyes on her?

But Wednesday she goes into Walton Park again. Peter Denham is still there, perched on the opened tailgate of the Fallen Arch, cracked boots up against one side. "Hello," Zoe says. She takes off her glasses. The world blurs.

"Hello," Peter says.

Zoe puts her glasses back on. "Peter, that's three days you've been sitting in the same place. That's long enough!"

She makes Peter laugh. Lord! Has she ever made any man laugh before?

He jumps up, rubbing his behind. "If you hadn't come along, I would have turned to stone. I was waiting for you."

"You were!"

"Sure."

Zoe feels herself reddening with pleasure. "Peter," she blurts, "the first day I saw you, Monday, I thought you were a mugger, or a rapist."

"Come on, Goldie, stop pulling my leg. You didn't think any such thing!"

"Yes! I did, I really did."

"You're a crazy kid!" He produces half a string of tough dried figs from inside the cooler. "Fig, Goldie?"

"I should really be going. My grandmother expects

me home." She wants to bite her tongue off. Why did she have to say that?

"Figs are good," Peter says, nibbling away. "A little hard on the teeth, maybe. Sure you won't have one?" His red beard is wiry, a bit skimpy.

"Oh, well—okay. Thank you." Zoe nibbles at the dried fruit.

"Sit down," Peter says, moving to make room for her. "Take that sack off your shoulders and stay awhile." He smiles, giving off an odor of mint and sweat. He tells her he's just brewed his own tea from wild mint he picks in the fields. "So, what's new?"

Because she's been thinking about it, she says, "My birthday's coming." At once she looks away, embarrassed at sounding so childish.

"Your birthday? When?"

"Saturday."

"Terrific. Which one?"

"Fourteen."

Peter shakes his head, smiling. "Wow, Goldie, you make me feel like an old man. Nineteen—the Ancient Mariner." He shakes his head again, and Zoe bursts out laughing, a free, happy laugh. Peter puts his arm around Zoe's shoulder and gives her a little hug. "You got any brothers or sisters?"

"Just me."

"No kidding!" She nods. "Listen, let me be your brother, and you can be my sister away from home." He says it sweetly. Zoe's face fills up with emotion.

After a moment she tells Peter about Ron and Don,

the twin brothers she made up when she was nine. Ron and Don were in the navy. Ron and Don sent Zoe a box of candy on Valentine's Day. Ron and Don made a special trip home to see her on Thanksgiving, and wrote her letters constantly.

"What happened to old Ron and Don?"

Zoe shakes her head. "Oh, the kids I knew, they just didn't believe me—"

"Aw, you should have let Ron and Don die a heroic death at sea, Goldie. You missed your chance."

Some kids on bikes pass, yelling. Peter talks about British Columbia in western Canada. "BC," Peter says, "like they say in the ads, a true unspoiled paradise. Oh, you have to see it!"

"I've never been anywhere in my life," Zoe bursts out.

"Oh, come on, sure you have, everyone's gone some-place."

"Nowhere. Never anywhere."

"Well, you must have made a trip sometime."

"We go to Cranberry Lake in the Adirondacks every summer for two weeks. Okay?"

"That'll do for a beginning," he says, smiling his grayish, touching smile. "And where else?"

Zoe shakes her head. "Nowhere."

"You sure?"

"Nowhere."

Peter looks at her curiously, then turns and scrounges around inside the wagon, returning with his sketchbook. He flips it open, turning the spiral-bound pages till he comes to the picture he wants. A rough charcoal sketch of Zoe walking away down the path through the park. There she is, thin as a straw, knapsacked, skinny-legged. Embarrassed, Zoe doesn't know what to say. How can she praise it? She looks as plain, as ordinary as she fears she is.

"I'm going to give you that for your birthday," Peter says. "It's going to be your birthday present, but first, I'm going to fix it up. Going to make this a road you're on, cars traveling along, a sign that says Arizona Highway 55." As he talks he's already rubbing out the park background with his thumb. "Traveling Zoe, I'm going to call it," he says with satisfaction. "You come here Saturday, okay?"

"Saturday? Sure."

"Tell you what. Come on over about eight o'clock, we'll have a birthday breakfast. English muffins, dates, and mint tea."

"Oh!" Zoe bites her lip. Every year on her birthday Marcia makes a special breakfast.

"You want to do that?" Peter says.

"I'd love to, but—"

"But nothing! It isn't every day you're fourteen." He hugs her.

"Okay," Zoe says. "Okay! I will." Somehow it will work out. She thinks back to her ignorant pre-knowing-Peter self. Imagine: if she had never gone into the park she would never have met Peter. The fine line between Peter-in-the-flesh and Peter-not-at-all makes Zoe shudder. Is all life so chancy?

41

When Zoe leaves a little later, Peter shouts after her, "Saturday!"

Zoe turns, walks backward. "Okay!" she yells back. "And maybe I'll see you tomorrow, too, okay?"

Peter raises thumb and forefinger in a circle.

Then Zoe starts running, runs all the way home. It's late. She's not sure how late, but she knows it's a lot later than she's ever come home before without an explanation.

And sure enough, the moment Zoe enters the kitchen, her grandmother says, "Where've you been?" She yanks a pan of food out of the oven. "You're late, Ducky."

"Sorry, Marcia. I was—uh—just walking."

"Walking? Where were you walking?"

"Nowhere." Zoe shakes her head, hunches her shoulders. "Noplace."

"Well, you got to walk someplace, Ducky," Marcia says reasonably. "Someplace to take so much time to get home."

"I was just mooching around."

"Mooching around?" Marcia repeats. "What's this? What's this *mooching* around?"

It's a word she's picked up from Peter. She feels the heat in her face. "Um, just walking slowly, I guess," she says.

Marcia lights a cigarette and lets it dangle from the corner of her mouth. She never inhales and likes to say, "I smoke like a chimney, but I'll never die of cancer."

"Walking slowly," Marcia says. "What do you mean, walking slowly, Ducky? What was to walk slowly about?"

"Nothing. I guess—um—" Zoe shrugs and smiles at Marcia.

"Were you walking with someone?" Marcia's brown eyes spark joyfully as she senses a little fight coming. "Ducky, don't turn your head like that, give Marcia an answer."

"I wasn't walking with anyone," Zoe says softly, trying to stick to the technical truth. She takes her schoolbooks out of her knapsack, looks at each one intently, as if she has nothing else in the world on her mind.

"Was a boy walking with you? Is my pretty ducky attracting boys now?"

"Marcia. I'm not pretty." Zoe adjusts her gold wire-framed glasses.

"Who says you're not pretty? What kind of talk is that? Has someone been telling you garbage about not being pretty?" Marcia looks ready now to fight the world, not Zoe.

"I can tell myself," Zoe says. "I'm not pretty." She raises her shoulders, lets them drop. "I can see that for myself, so can you. I'm not pretty. Okay?"

"I don't want you thinking negatively about yourself, Ducky. Pretty is as pretty does!"

"I know," Zoe says. She waits for Marcia to add, Beauty is skin deep.

Marcia blows smoke through her nose. "Beauty is skin deep," Marcia says. "Think about that."

"Okay," Zoe says.

Maybe beauty is skin deep and pretty is as pretty

does, but some people have *something*, and some people don't. Zoe knows she doesn't, while Mama does. Elegant Mama, stylish Weezy. Even Marcia, though neither elegant nor stylish, has such crackling energy that wherever she goes she is noticed.

And Zoe? Next to the three women, she often feels like a negative, faint, dim—a grayish splotch against their vivid background.

"So, who is the lucky boy?" Marcia says.

"Huh?"

"Zoe, don't say huh."

"I know. I'm sorry."

"Huh sounds stupid."

"I know."

"Did he walk you home?"

Zoe's lips firm. She's not going to talk about Peter. "Marcia, no boy walked me home."

"You're awful late, Ducky, there's gotta be a reason."

Later, at the dinner table, along with the tuna fish casserole, Marcia serves up Zoe's late homecoming.

"Bet she's got a boyfriend," Weezy says, bracelets clinking. "Zoey? Come on, no secrets now."

"Sly Boots isn't talking," Marcia says.

"Why shouldn't she have a boyfriend?" Mama says. "Plenty of boys are going to break their hearts over Zoe, before long."

"Look at her there with that smile on her face," Weezy says. "Oh, she's got secrets, she's got secrets."

"Wonder who he could be?" Marcia says, vigorously forking up her food. "What's his name? Jimmy? Johnny?

Marshall?" They repeat delightedly that she was just "mooching around."

"Mooching rhymes with smooching," Marcia says.

"Smooching?" Zoe says. And they all laugh. Mama's eyes sparkle, she looks wonderful when she laughs.

"Don't tell me this generation doesn't know about smooching," Marcia says. "Oh, my, what do the young people do today?"

"Ask me no questions, Mother, I'll tell you no lies," Weezy sings. "They just move in together, that's about it, or else share a mattress."

"Weezy, that's vulgar," Mama protests, looking at Zoe.

The bantering, joyful and persistent, goes on, surrounding Zoe like a soft woolly blanket, familiar, comforting, binding. They're all smiling, relaxed; they lean in toward her, radiating their love like little fires in the dark. Weezy reaches for the last cinnamon bun, then pushes it toward Zoe. Mama strokes her hair, her hand soft, soothing, making Zoe feel sleepy, yet faintly irritable.

"Zoe isn't going to be late anymore, is she?" Marcia says, leaning back comfortably with her first after-dinner cigarette.

"But—" Zoe presses her lips together.

"But what?" Weezy says. "But—but—but—but I want to 'mooch around,' the girl says!"

"Oh no, she doesn't. Just had spring fever today. Tomorrow she'll be all cooled off." And Marcia, who started the whole brouhaha, ends it by saying, "Now let's leave her alone, we're going to wear her right out with this nonsense."

And it's true, Zoe feels unaccountably weary, and goes to bed early. When she's half asleep, Mama comes in and leans over her. "Sweetie," she says, half whispering, "you know if there is a boy—"

"What?" Zoe mumbles sleepily.

"I don't want you to have secrets from me, sweetie. I love you, I don't want you to be hurt."

"I know." Zoe almost says, *Mama, I met Peter in Walton Park—* She closes her eyes. Mama puts cool fingers on Zoe's eyes. "Sleep well." She tiptoes out, shutting the door quietly. The room is dark. Beyond, Zoe hears the comfortable noises of the house, familiar and soothing.

Now she is wakeful again. She thinks about Peter. Behind that red beard does he have a weak soft chin like Richie Eberhardt? Is there something a little crazy about a man living in a station wagon? She rolls over on her back, puts her hand to her chest. Her heart seems to be pounding right up into her throat. Maybe *she's* crazy, breaking the rules, making friends with a total stranger, a vagrant, a vagabond, a nineteen-year-old drifter and loafer.

After a while, she falls asleep, but wakes suddenly from a horrible nightmare: Someone is throwing a knife at Mama, she sees it flying through the air, sees red blood on Mama's white linen dress. It takes her a long time to fall asleep again.

Thursday morning, Marcia is singing in the kitchen, Weezy is in the shower, but Mama doesn't get out of bed. Zoe goes to her room. "What's the matter?"

"Migraine," Mama says in a weak voice. Her room is darkened, there's a damp towel across her forehead, her face is bled of color. Zoe strokes her hand helplessly. Mama tries to smile. "I ate chocolate," she whispers. "Isn't that stupid and greedy? Whole chocolate almond bar yesterday." Mama's migraines are triggered strangely. Allergies to chocolate and fish can bring on the devastating pain, or a worry, or seemingly nothing.

"Poor Mama, poor Mama," Zoe says, kissing her cheek. What can she do to take away the pain? She feels as sad, as sorry, as guilty as if she caused the raging storm in Mama's head. By "mooching around," by deception, by half-lies, and ugly dreams. "I'll be home right after school," she says, stroking the limp hand. "Right home. Okay? You rest and try to feel better." She adjusts the shade, smooths the covers, lingers for a moment, then leaves.

After school she goes resolutely home, walks past Walton Park's stone gates. She closes her eyes and makes a tiny prayer, an offering. *I won't see Peter, okay? So, in return, please take Mama's headache away.*

On Friday, Mama is almost recovered from the migraine, but she stays home from work feeling weak, drained. Zoe promises to bring her peach ice cream after school. She veers briskly around Walton Park. Still can't allow herself to see Peter. Mama isn't all better yet. Tomorrow, though, she promises herself.

She stops in the little corner grocery and, besides the peach ice cream, she buys a rubber troll with wispy white hair. Mama has collected these grotesque little dolls for a long time.

"Oh, no, not another one," Marcia says when Zoe produces it. Marcia hates the trolls lined up on Mama's bureau and threatens to throw them all out. Mama always says, "You give up cigarettes, Mother, and I'll get rid of the trolls. Word of honor." It's a standoff.

Waking on Saturday morning, Zoe opens her eyes and thinks at once of Peter. She promised she'd be there by eight, and it's already ten minutes past. From the kitchen she hears Marcia, busy with the whirring blender. In the other bed Weezy sits up and smiles. "Happy birthday, Zoey!"

Zoe gets up, pulls on her jeans. If she runs she can still be there in time. But in the kitchen there's a stack of gaily ribboned packages laid by her plate and Marcia waiting to make blueberry pancakes. "You always want blueberry pancakes on your birthday," Marcia says, hugging her. And Zoe, for the third year in a row, can't tell Marcia that she no longer adores blueberry pancakes that much. And can't find the courage, either, to disappoint them all and say she wants to go out for a while.

"Happy birthday, happy birthday, happy birthday to you, happy birthday, darling Zoe," Mama sings, sitting down at the table. Mama looks fresh, creamy, completely recovered. She squeezes Zoe's hand. "It's going to be a wonderful year for you."

Weezy, wearing her red velvet robe tied at the middle, pours syrup over her pancakes. "I gave Zoe my birthday wishes already." Reminding the others that these days she, alone, is privileged to share early mornings with Zoe.

Zoe stares at the mound of pancakes with their little blue bubbles, like blue pimples. She looks up at the clock over the refrigerator. It's nine o'clock.

"Open your presents, Zoey," Weezy says eagerly.

Slowly Zoe unwraps the first present, a leather-bound address book from Mama. "It's beautiful. I love it." She looks around at their waiting, joyful faces and sinks down in her chair, opening the next present. There's a turquoise ring from Weezy, a comb and brush set, scarves, a graceful porcelain cat for her cat shelf. "Mother, that must have cost a little fortune," Weezy says, stroking the sleek, shining back of the cat. "Porcelain!"

Marcia juts out her chin satisfiedly. "I found it at a house sale. You don't mind, Ducky?"

"I love it," Zoe says again.

All day it's Zoe's day. They don't leave her alone or forget her for a minute. No chance ever to get away. Take her out to lunch, then to a movie. They eat popcorn and jelly beans in the movie and whisper back and forth to each other. They have a steak dinner, big baked Idaho potatoes, and chocolate cake with candles and more singing of Happy Birthday. And finally, her big present, a ten-speed European bike that Weezy, smiling gloriously, pedals into the living room.

"Surprise! Surprise!"

Zoe gets on her new bike and rides it in circles around the living room.

"It's been a lovely day," Mama says.

"Perfect," Weezy agrees. "A wonderful birthday. And I am utterly pooped."

"We didn't forget a thing," Marcia says with satisfaction.

In the middle of the night Zoe wakes up, terrified, from a half-remembered dream. Something about an accident, bodies on the road. She thinks she dreamt that Mama, Weezy, and Marcia were all in a terrible accident. All dead. Her throat pulses. She still remembers the last words of the dream, but can't make sense of them. *Oh, no you don't.*

She lies rigid, staring into the darkness. There are oceans pounding in her ears. The darkness is like filthy water. She gasps for breath. It's impossible to stay in bed. She stumbles to the bathroom, turns on the light, and sits on the toilet seat. And there she is overcome with grief, senseless, profound, irresistible grief. She sobs wretchedly. She thinks of Peter waiting for her, waiting all day. She chokes back her sobs. If they hear her, they will all come running. She washes her face with cold water, douses her eyes. *Peter*, she thinks. She wants to see Peter.

She gazes, nearsighted and astonished, at her own reflection. Peter? Yes. And now. She wants to see him *right now.*

She goes to her room, fetches her light coat from the closet and puts it on over her short nightgown. All this coming and going and clattering has finally brought Weezy awake. She sits up, switches on her bedside lamp, and stares at Zoe. "What are you doing?"

Zoe says nothing. She is incapable of speech. Only one thought. *I'm going to see Peter.* She glances back at Weezy as she leaves the room. Without makeup, Weezy's face looks flattened, as if seen through layers of water.

Zoe walks swiftly through the dark house. As she opens the door she hears them behind her, all of them, crying in confusion. "Zoe, wait! . . . Zoe, you can't . . . Ducky! . . . Zoey . . . come back here, Zoe baby! . . ."

She is out on the street. A light rain is falling. She walks swiftly. Will Mama come after her in the car? Why didn't she take her new bicycle? She turns a corner, another. It is crazy, crazy, and yet she feels perfectly calm, sensible, and sane. She is going to see Peter, that's all there is to it. She's going to see her friend. It's her birthday and she hasn't seen her friend yet. So be quiet, Mama! Be quiet, Weezy and Marcia! This is just something I have to do.

She's never been out so late at night. The streets are deserted. She thinks it must be one or two, maybe even three o'clock. Not even a dog barking. Far away there's a hum from the highway. She's never heard the city so quiet. She hurries past the darkened houses. Only then does she notice that her feet are bare. The cool, gritty, slightly dampened sidewalk feels pleasant.

She goes down another street. No one has seen her. No one has stopped her. Her mind begins to hum pleasantly. She will knock on the window of the wagon to wake Peter, gently knock, so as not to frighten him. He told her once about being wakened from a deep sleep by police who made him move his wagon then and there, didn't even allow him time to put on a pair of shoes. Peter will sit up, fuzzy-eyed, rub his red beard, then smile as he makes out her face in the light from the park lamps. *You! Goldie, what are you doing here?*

I couldn't get away this morning, but I'm here now.

You sure are! He'll snap his fingers. *Was I sorry you didn't come. I had everything ready for our celebration.*

I'm sorry I broke my promise to you, Peter. But here I am, anyway.

In the middle of the night? You nutty kid! But he'll be grinning. He'll open the tailgate. *Look at you, barefooted. Come on in.*

She'll climb into the wagon, sit on his mattress, shivering and smiling. Peter will put a blanket around her, then his arm. *What a nutty little sister*, he'll say, hugging her. And he'll kiss her on the cheek, then on the lips.

Zoe walks faster as she enters the park gates. Her feet scrunch on the gravel path and she veers off to the grass. Her hair, freed from the daytime braids, floats around her shoulders. The park lamps are all haloed with mist. The moon, thin as a slice of peach, shows fuzzily for a moment, then disappears behind a cloud.

She rushes up to Peter's trees. She thinks it's his tree, the blasted pine. No, she's *sure* it's his tree. But . . . the station wagon isn't there. She frowns, blinks, sniffs, wipes her hand across her nose. The station wagon is gone. Peter is gone.

Zoe's mind stumbles over this plain fact, unable to take it in. How can he be gone? Where is he? She must have come to the wrong place then. She rushes up the path, but turns back. No, she knows where the wagon was parked, and now it's gone. It isn't there. It's vanished.

No, it didn't vanish. He drove it away.

Drove it away. Those three words penetrate.

"Peter," she calls into the blackness beyond the park lights. "Peter?"

There's no answer.

She's all alone in the middle of the night in Walton Park.

She scuffs around on the ground, getting a little scared now, but not willing to leave. Maybe Peter will come back. Maybe she will find something of his. Maybe he left her a secret message. Maybe . . . there's a crumpled cigarette package under a bush. She snatches it up. *Warning. The Surgeon General* . . . Is it Peter's? Did he smoke? Maybe smoking is against his religion? She thinks of the small gold cross around his neck. She knows that's a stupid thought. She throws away the cigarette package.

She thinks she hears something in the bushes. She stiffens, listens. It comes to her then that she's alone in Walton Park at night, and it could be dangerous.

She trots back through the park, moving steadily, her breath puffing in her ears. As she passes between the stone gates and out onto Court Place, a car passes, a head turns to stare. Zoe continues trotting, and is soon home.

The house is blazing with lights. Lights in every window. The car is gone from the driveway. Mama is out looking for her, and Weezy and her grandmother are waiting.

"She's here, she's back, Zoe is back," Weezy cries, as if Marcia can't see her. "Zoey's here! My God, where were you? Where did you go? Your mother is out driving around this city, crying her eyes out, looking for you. My God."

Marcia, a cigarette dangling from her lower lip, takes Zoe by the shoulders, brushes her hair, pinches her face between her hands, blows smoke into Zoe's face. "Are you crazy?" Marcia says. "Running out in the middle of the night like that?"

Zoe is terribly tired. She seems to see Weezy and Marcia as if through the wrong end of a telescope, from a great distance. Even their voices seem to come to her from a distance. And when Mama enters the house a moment later, she, too, is very far away.

Mama says nothing but hugs Zoe and then looks into her face. She wants Zoe to tell, to explain. They are all looking at her, waiting for her to speak. She has caused them hours of terror. She had made them all suffer needlessly.

She thinks of saying, Peter is gone. But then they will cry, *Peter? Who is Peter?* Their voices will rise in alarm, they will surround her with questions, and love, and worry. So she says nothing.

She thinks, *One day I walked into Walton Park and I met Peter, who was sitting on the back of his green station wagon.* "Now then—!" Marcia begins again. If anyone can, she will get the long and the short of this extraordinary episode out of Zoe. *He was my friend. We talked. We laughed about things.* "You explain yourself!"

Marcia demands. *One night I went back into Walton Park, and Peter was gone.*

"Sweetie, please," Mama says.

Peter, I went back to see you. I was late, but I went to see you, Peter. Come back, Peter. You will come back.

"Zoe darling," Weezy implores.

Zoe rubs her arms. "You're chilled," Marcia says, aggravated. "Running around in bare feet. I don't understand you. You're going to catch cold. You know how susceptible you are!"

"You'll have to have hot tea and aspirin," Weezy says.

They crowd around her, touch her. "Zoe, darling!" they murmur, and wait for her to speak, explain, reassure, to become once again their good Zoe whom, all her life, they have protected, adored, and known like the pages of a much-read and well-loved book.

But Zoe says nothing. There's nothing for her to say. What she's done, she's done, and what she'll do in the future only she knows. She shakes out her hair. She loves them all dearly, but she can't remain their little Zoe forever. Don't they know that? She kisses Mama, she hugs Weezy, rubs her cheeks against Marcia's.

"Good night," she says. "Good night." She is fourteen, she did what she meant to do, and to tell the truth, she feels, quite simply, splendid.

Something Expensive

About a month before I took the Scotty route, my mother gave me a watch. That was in October, the same month Colin and I decided to go together. The watch had a small white face with blue numbers, and a blue wristband. I knew it was expensive, I'd seen it in the window of Wilson's Jewelers for close to sixty dollars. I wore it all the time. I took it off only at night, and during the day I'd put it to my ear five, or six, or maybe ten times just to hear it ticking. TICKTICKTICKtickticktickticktick . . . like a heartbeat. I don't know why I loved the watch's heartbeat so much, but listening to it gave me the same sort of rushing, happy feeling I got when my mother came into the house evenings after work, putting down packages, hugging James, talking to me, giving everyone orders.

Well, yes, I felt happy about the watch, but it also upset me a little. Because it was so unusual for Mom to give me anything. She hardly ever gave me or James presents, not even on our birthdays. Some people think that's awful, but I never minded. My mother is like a gift herself. You only have to be around her for a little while to see what I mean.

In its own way, taking the Scotty route was another funny thing. I didn't understand myself exactly. As my father pointed out, in summer and in fall when it would have been nice and pleasant weather for a newspaper route, I never gave it a thought. Then, in November, with dark coming earlier, there I was delivering Scottys. The Scotty comes out once a week. It's a little half-size pulp newspaper with no news, only ads for garage sales, furniture, cars, baby-sitting, and also public announcements. PANCAKE BREAKFAST TO RAISE MONEY FOR HOLY CROSS BASKETBALL TEAM, ALL YOU CAN EAT FOR $2. BRING THE WHOLE FAMILY. Or, JEWISH COMMUNITY CENTER WILL HOLD YOGA CLASSES FOR TIRED BUSINESSMEN AT 5:30, IN-STRUCTOR BABE SWERDLOW, LEARN TO RELAX THROUGH PROPER BREATHING AND ANCIENT EXERCISES.

Once, before I worked for them, my mother put an ad in the Scotty. I called it into the Scotty office for her. "For sale, mouton coat size 7, good condition, reasonable, call 446-2247 after 6."

Dad didn't want her to sell the mouton. "It's warmer than a regular wool coat," he said, pushing his fingers through the stiff fur. "And up here with these winters, you need a warm coat. You know how cold you get, your feet and all."

"I don't wear the coat on my feet," Mom said.

We all laughed. I know it's not the funniest remark in the world, but there's something about Mom, the way she says things, that makes you laugh. Anyway, she said Dad was actually right about the coat being warm. And it was waterproof, too. "But I can't stand it," she said. "Listen, my sister Grace had it when she went to nursing school back in the fifties. And even then, even when it was new, every time it rained, it smelled like wet cat."

"Wet cat! Oooh, barf!" James said, doubling over with his hands clutching his stomach. James is very dramatic. He's more like Mom. I'm more like Dad. We're both tall and blond, sort of slow, and neat, and not too fast to get angry.

"Besides," Mom said, "I am not a fur-coat type. Right, Marylee?" she said, to me. "Admit it, I look ridiculous in a fur coat. Fur-coat types are long, and lean, and *sweep* into rooms."

Mom is anything but long and lean, and the way she rushes into rooms, with a dozen things to tell you, she certainly doesn't make regal entrances. So many times I've seen Dad smiling and shaking his head at Mom, as if he just couldn't believe her.

Anyway, the Scotty ad for the mouton coat cost one dollar, and about a dozen people called on it. I took most of the calls and had fun telling everyone what a good coat it was. Mom sold it for twenty dollars and bought us all ice skates with the money. I was eleven then, and James was three. (James got those double runners with little red laces.) Mom wanted to buy Dad a pair of ice skates, too, but he wouldn't hear of it. "I'd fall flat on my ass," he said.

"Would you?" Mom said. "How do you know?"

"I'm too old to start ice skating again. I gave it up, or rather it gave me up about a dozen years ago, and that's it."

"Oh! Old-Bick-in-the-Mud," Mom said. That was one of her pet names for Dad then. He is Bickford Daniels, Jr. (He wanted to name James, Bickford Daniels III, but Mom said, "I'd rather name my baby, Baby Boy XYZ than stick him with Bick-ford Dan-e-els the Third. The poor kid, imagine dragging a load like that around for the rest of his life.")

For a long time I haven't heard my mother tease my father about his name, or call him Old-Bick-in-the-Mud. And I haven't seen my father giving my mother that puzzled, pleased smile and headshake like, Wow, where did I get such a tiny, lively wife! In fact, ever since that day last fall when Mom climbed up into the maple tree and sat there for a couple hours, saying she had to think about things, Dad hadn't smiled at all. When Mom did come down out of the tree, he refused to talk to her. He wouldn't come to supper, either, just plunked himself down in a corner of the living room with his racing-car magazines. He has a huge collection of racing-car magazines, most of them stacked up in the cellar. He saves every issue, and he's been getting them for, oh, I don't know, maybe fifteen years? Maybe more. Probably more, now that I think of it, because he's been crazy about racing cars since he was a boy. I guess he really wanted to be a racing-car driver, but he isn't. He drives a panel truck for Rastoni's, delivering grocery orders. Before he worked for Rastoni's, he drove a truck for City Dry Cleaners over on East Avenue. Then, a do-it-yourself cleaning place moved in right next to City Dry Cleaners and they went out of business. Anyway, Rastoni's is a better job because people tip him, and he can pick up food bargains. We're not poor, but we don't have a huge amount of money, either. My mother is a telephone company supervisor, a good job; she makes about the same money as my father. I get an allowance and do some baby-sitting. And now I also make three dollars a week on the Scotty route.

My father was opposed to my taking the route. "A girl shouldn't be out on the streets alone when it's dark," he said.

"Ridiculous," my mother said. "She's always out on the streets alone, anytime she goes to visit a friend—"

"She doesn't have to work," my father said. "I'll raise her allowance."

"No," my mother said. "Money doesn't solve everything! She wants to do this, let her. People have to do things. You can't chain people down, Bick, you can't turn off people's desires."

I tried to put in that it wasn't the money, but they weren't listening. They were quarreling again. Sometimes, I tried to figure when the fighting had started, but I never could decide. They'd always had little squabbles— doesn't everybody?—but these were different, real fights.

All through the fall they were fighting two or three times a week. James took up sucking his thumb again, Mom started working lots of overtime, and I decided to do the Scotty.

I was surprised to find out how much I liked doing the route. I liked the way the sack of folded, rubber-banded papers grew lighter with each delivery. I liked tucking each paper carefully into a protected spot on the porch or behind the storm door.

It was peaceful cutting across the white lawns, looking into lighted windows, seeing people inside for just a moment, then passing on. Once, I saw a man staring out the window. He was standing by a huge, leafy green plant (I couldn't tell if it was real or artificial), and although he was inside he was wearing a hat. Another time, I saw a family sitting around a table, eating. A chandelier spilled a dome of pale buttery light down on them. And then, once, I saw three kids through a window, dancing with their arms up in the air. The room was blue from the TV. It was like a snapshot, or maybe a moment in a play. Somehow perfect, everything exactly as it should be. As I hurried past the window (I never wanted to linger, I only wanted to see that frozen instant), I could feel my heart beating like my watch—ticktickticktickticktick—and it was so odd, I felt so happy because I'd seen those three kids dancing.

Walking in the cold and the dark, listening to the crackle of slush or frozen snow beneath my boots, was a good time to think about things, about school and friends, and Colin Lambert.

I'd known Colin forever, but we'd only started going together after Franny Klake's Halloween party.

I wasn't even planning to go to Franny's party. They were always the same, all the girls came, but never enough boys. But then I was glad I did go, because Colin was there, and for some reason it was different this time. We started talking and we stayed together for the whole party. Colin's about my size, sort of wiry, with glasses and nice brown eyes.

After that we began eating lunch together every day in school, and on weekends we went to the movies, or fooled around at the shopping center with some of the other kids. All of those kids were going together, and Colin and I fit right in.

I liked Colin a lot, I really did, and you like to be positive with the people you like, so the few things I didn't care for about him I kept quiet about. Such as copying. After we started going together, Colin was always copying my homework, and a few times he even copied answers to science tests. Well, the truth is, I hate people to copy homework and test papers. I work pretty hard to get decent marks in school, it doesn't come all that easily, and then—well, you know, to have someone just take so casually what I've worked for, it hurts. But the fact of the matter is, I have never stopped anyone from copying my homework and my test papers.

This was one of the things I thought about on the route—this, and my parents' quarrels.

They were quarreling again the night I had to write

a composition for my English teacher. "Describe the members of your family and how they interact," Mrs. Shore had said earlier in the day when she gave the assignment. She wore big purple-tinted glasses and had long streaky blond hair. "Try to give the *feeling* of your family, the *ambience*, the *vibrations*," she told us.

The vibrations were bad that night. One of our neighbors had borrowed my father's Phillips screwdriver and never returned it. Then Dad needed the Phillips for a job around the house, but instead of asking Mr. Ferrari, he'd gone out and bought a new one. I knew why he did it. The same reason I never said anything when Colin copied my work.

But it made my mother mad. "For God's sake, Bick, that man has had the Phillips for six months. Why didn't you just ask him for it?"

"Well, if he was ready to return it, he would have returned it," my father said.

"You let people take advantage of you."

"It wasn't that much money." Dad is big and fair, and when he quarrels with Mom, he flushes like he's embarrassed, or shy, or something.

"It's not the money, it's the idea," Mom said. "The *principle*. It's your screwdriver, not his. Why should he have it? Why didn't you assert yourself!"

"Oh, well now . . . well, now," Dad said, and he pulled down his lower lip, something he always does when he has nothing else to say, when no matter how my mother argues, yells, or pleads, he won't say another word. He

just retreats, goes silent, picks up his racing-car magazine, and starts reading. But first he pulls down his lower
lip, pulls it like a piece of stretched-out rubber.

"Stop that," my mother said, her face getting dark.
"Stop that! Stop doing that! You do that just to infuriate
me." And she picked up the little green velvet throw
pillows from the couch and flung them both at Dad.

About an hour later, it was quiet again. My mother had
gone out, my father was reading, and James was in bed,
so I sat down to write my composition. All lies, I knew
it was all lies, but what could I do?

I began like this. "It's evening, the TV is on. My father
is sitting on the couch with my little brother, James,
next to him. My mother is knitting a sweater for me—
she says she'll knit one for Dad next—and I'm sitting at
the dining-room table with my schoolbooks open. This
is the way my family spends a typical evening at home."

Maybe I'd seen a family like this through one of the
lighted windows on my route. A perfect moment in a
perfect family. The trouble was, I couldn't get past that
one picture. I managed to write a few more sentences,
but then I had to end it. I wasn't too surprised when
Mrs. Shore gave me B over C. B for penmanship, spell-
ing, grammar, etc., and C for content.

In January, my mother started working even more
hours at the phone company, coming home late several
nights a week. Dad, James, and I would eat supper
together, and it was always awful without her. I didn't
even feel hungry. Sometimes she came home only in time
to do the dishes with me. For years, she and I have

done the dishes together at night. She washes and I dry, and she talks to me about when she was a girl, and her work, and what I should do in the future. She always tells me to go to college, to become a teacher, or a scientist, or even a lawyer.

"I only went to college for one year, then I got married, but you'll be educated, Marylee, and that counts for a whole lot. It counts! Doesn't it, Bick?" she called to my father one night.

"What?" He was reading his magazine.

"I want Marylee to be educated. I want her to take her life in her own hands!"

"Don't give her so many ideas, leave her alone," he said.

"You want her to be a slug!" my mother called.

"Don't talk stupid. Just leave people alone."

"Do you hear yourself?" She went to the kitchen door, dripping soapsuds on the floor. "Do you hear yourself saying that? I think that's very good advice! Yes, leave people alone!"

I dried dishes furiously, in my mind taking first his side, then hers, then his again. I knew I preferred my mother, and this made me feel ashamed, disloyal to Dad. I wanted to be impartial, to love him as much as her. But the truth was, I didn't. I loved him very much, yes! but not the way I loved her. The way I loved her was just—like a hopeless passion. Sometimes I thought, Who would I be, what would I be, without her? Not just that she had given birth to me. More than that. I wanted to be like her. Of course, I never could in looks. I was tall and fair like my father, not small and dark like her, but in other ways, I could try to be like her. Whenever I was around her, I laughed more easily, felt myself expanding, opening, I moved more quickly the way she did, and I remembered to walk with my arms swinging and my head up.

The quarrels continued through January and February. My father didn't say anything about her working more hours. Instead he'd pick at her for forgetting to buy tissues, or not bagging the garbage properly, or because he didn't have a pair of clean socks. "This is stupid, stupid," she would yell. My father never yelled. He would talk for a long time, telling her all the things she did wrong around the house. His face would flush and pale, flush and pale. Then, when she got mad enough to yell, he would pull at his lower lip and walk away from her and not talk anymore.

It was freezing every day in February. We had an ice storm. There was slick polished ice everywhere, on the streets and sidewalks, a layer of ice like frosting on every car, and all the trees and telephone wires sagged under ice. Sometimes I thought the freezing air from outside was slipping into our house through invisible cracks, punctures, holes and leaks; the furnace worked and worked, but there was always a cold draft leaking in somewhere.

One night when I got home from school, the kitchen was dark. Nothing had been touched since breakfast. Dirty dishes in the sink, cocoa smeared on the stove, bread crumbs on the counter, a fork on the floor. "Mom?"

I called, but I knew she wasn't home. The house felt different without her.

"Not home," James said, popping in from the living room. He had his thumb jammed in his mouth like it was a magic lollipop.

"Take the thumb out." I ran hot water in the sink and poured in liquid detergent. Pink bubbles floated into the air.

"Do you know how many more days to my birthday?" James said.

"Of course I do."

"How many?"

"Enough." I left the dishes soaking and opened the refrigerator. My mother had left hamburger patties on a plate covered with Saran Wrap.

"What are you getting me for a present? I bet you're not getting me anything."

"When did I ever forget your birthday?"

"Uh—uh—last year when I was younger."

"Dumbo. I got you your magic blackboard last year."

"Oh, yeah."

"Oh, yeah, yourself."

"Making supper now?" He pulled up his shirt and rubbed his belly. "I'm *starved!*"

"Take the milk and ketchup out of the refrig." I stuck the patties under the broiler.

"Mom working overtime again?" I asked Dad when he came out of the bathroom. He was freshly shaved and showered. He likes to do that every day after work. He had on clean pants and a fresh shirt.

"I suppose," he said. He plucked at his lower lip, and smiled a little. Even his smile upset me. It flickered on and off on his face like a light bulb that's almost going out. I wanted to shout like my mother did, Don't do that!

"Mama works overtime every day," James said.

"Not yesterday!" I said sharply. "She was home yesterday. Remember?"

"No," James said.

"Yes, you do! Don't you remember, for supper we had —we had—" Suddenly, I couldn't remember. I wasn't sure if Mom had been home or not. Maybe James was right. There was a lump in my stomach, I didn't feel hungry, but I took the hamburgers off the broiler and put them on the table. I was sick of hamburgers, and for no reason at all I thought I might cry.

After supper I cleared the table and started on the dishes, doing the ones from breakfast, too. I worked slowly, listening for my mother's car in the driveway, hoping she would come in. I knew just how she'd sound and look when she rushed in, her cheeks bright from the cold, her dark hair messy, clapping her hands together, calling out to each one of us. "Bick," she'd call, "how are you? How was work? James, what happened in school today?" Then she'd come into the kitchen, she'd pull a dish towel around her waist and shove me away from the sink, saying, "Oh, you did plenty tonight, honey. More than enough. God, what would I do without you? Those two men in there—helpless!" We'd both laugh, then she'd tell me again to go and relax, do something else. But I'd stay and work with her, I'd tell her about school, maybe I'd mention Colin sitting next to me in assembly, I'd tell her about the A I'd received on a math paper. "No kidding!" she'd say. "Marylee, you are going to do fine things in the world!"

All the time I was washing the dishes, I kept making up the things my mother and I would say to each other. I dried the dishes and put them away in the cupboard and wiped up the counters, then swept the floor, and she still wasn't home.

Later, very late, I heard my mother coming up the steps and going into her bedroom. I fell asleep then and had a dream about my mother chasing away a pack of dogs. I woke up, remembering something real from a long time ago. I'd been seven or eight, coming home from school, and suddenly a gang of older boys surrounded me, penned me in. I couldn't get away. One of the boys stroked my head. The others laughed. I was terrified. They were saying things.

All at once, my mother was there. She pushed the boys aside. "Shame on you!"

She was half the size of those boys. Any one of them could have knocked her down easily. But when she yelled at them they ran away.

Remembering all that, for some reason I started crying and pulled the pillow over my face, so no one would hear me.

In the morning my eyes felt tired and sandy. My mother was sleeping late, she didn't have to be at work till ten o'clock. I helped James with his breakfast, boiling an egg for him. My father drank coffee standing up by

69

the cupboard. It was snowing outside again, a thin gray snowfall, and even before I went out, I felt chilled and sad.

At lunchtime in school, Colin and I ate sitting under the first-floor stairwell. I had a tuna fish sandwich. I gave Colin half. Usually I looked forward to lunch, but that day my stomach felt full in a sickish way. "I wonder if I'm getting the flu."

"You got a temperature?" Colin said. "Stick out your tongue." Sometimes when we were fooling around and got silly, we pretended to play doctor the way kids do when they're about nine years old.

"No, it's my stomach. It feels queer, kind of like jelly. You know, quivery?"

"Give me the science homework," Colin said. "I didn't get a chance to do it."

I took another bite of tuna sandwich. It tasted awful, like something swept off the floor.

"Hey, you all right?" Colin gave me a friendly jab in the ribs and reached past me to pick up my notebook. "In here?" I nodded slowly, fighting that quivering sickness. Colin found my paper and scribbled the answers into his own notebook. "Okay, thanks," he said, snapping my notebook shut.

"I'll do the same for you someday, Marylee."

I smiled dutifully. I liked Colin a whole lot when we were walking home from school, talking, or when we went to the movies, and I liked some of the things that happened when we were kissing, but . . . but . . .

70

Something Expensive

"Want to do something after school?"

"I have to deliver my Scottys," I said.

"I'll come with you."

"No, don't." I looked down at my wristwatch, and again I felt that sickish, quivering, jelly-like sensation low behind my ribs. I didn't want Colin with me tonight. I put the watch to my ear. Tickticktick . . . TICK-TICKTICKTICK . . . I felt as if my heart were racing to keep up with the watch.

Later that evening, after I did my Scotty route, instead of going straight home, I walked down North Street, past the cemetery, toward the shopping center. Maybe I'd find something to buy for James's birthday. Where North intersected Seneca Boulevard, there were dozens of stores. I looked into the lit windows, checking out the toys, a huge panda bear, a miniature chess set, an airplane construction kit. I couldn't settle on anything. I didn't feel sorted out, calm, as I usually did after doing my route. I paused in front of Cubby's Ice Creameria, a funny place that served weird varieties of ice cream and where the owner, Cubby, kept a changing assortment of driftwood in the window. He'd tie bits of colored ribbon to the driftwood, set tiny plastic cowboys astride them, and scatter miniature sheep or dwarfish little toy frogs in niches. It was always fun looking in Cubby's window. I glanced up into the almost empty store and saw my mother.

My mother? I was so surprised. I squinted, pressing my face against the window. Yes, it was her sitting on one of the white plastic stools, half turned away from the counter. She wore her blue coat trimmed with fur at the collar and cuffs.

"Hey, Mom," I called, raising my hand to tap on the plate-glass window. Then I stopped. She wasn't alone. A man was with her. A stranger, someone I'd never seen before. He had a thick mustache and looked bulky in a light-colored overcoat. They were turned toward each other, my mother sitting up very straight, her head rising from her fur collar like a dark lovely flower.

The man's fur hat lay between them on the white counter. Their hands were touching. My mother threw back her head and laughed. I knew exactly how that laugh sounded. The man smiled, picked up his fur hat and put it on my mother's head, tipping it down over her eye. She leaned toward him and they kissed.

All those nights when she came home late. All those quarrels with my father. All those lies.

"Dear, do you know what time it is?" A woman, red-nosed from the cold, spoke to me. Speechless, I gaped at her, then ran down the street. The freezing air cut like little knives into my sinuses. I put my bare hands to my forehead. Where were my mittens? Not in my pockets. Gone. Lost? Stolen?

At home my father was waiting for supper. He smiled so normally. "You're a little late, Marylee. I get worried about you."

"I was looking for a present for James. His birthday—" I opened the refrigerator and at once felt dizzy, nauseous. "I can't make supper. I'm sick."

"Sick? What's the matter?"

"I don't know, my stomach. Maybe the flu—"

"You really feel sick? Why don't you lie down. James and I will have my scrambled eggs special." He sounded disappointed. He didn't like to cook.

"I'm sorry." I went upstairs to my room. I lay down, then got up. I sat on the edge of the bed. Just sat there. I kept seeing my mother and that man in Cubby's together. Maybe I'd imagined the whole thing. Was that possible? I wanted to ask somebody, was it possible to make up something so that you were positive you really saw it, and yet you didn't? Sometimes dreams were that real.

The room grew dark. I didn't move. Patterns of light from outside moved over the walls. Downstairs, the front door slammed. I heard my mother coming in, speaking to my father. Water ran in the pipes. The television was on. Then James came upstairs, singing to himself. "Twenty-one bottles of beer . . ." Where'd he learn that? Probably on the school bus. He went into the bathroom, started running water into the tub. "Nineteen bottles of beer on the wall . . ."

My mother knocked on the door. "Marylee? You sleeping, hon?"

"No."

"Can I come in? Your dad says you don't feel well." She opened the door and turned on the light. The sudden brightness made me wince. She bent over me, touched my cheeks. "Why were you sitting in the dark? Marylee, what's the matter?" She sat down next to me.

She was wearing silver hoop earrings, thin silver chains looped around her neck. She put her arm around me and tried to slide me next to her, tried to pull my head down against her, but I wouldn't let her. "Hey, Marylee— what is it?"

I wanted to say *I saw you*, but I couldn't get out one word. I was such a coward. I turned my head away. I felt horrible, as if I were burning up.

"Are you getting a virus? You better hop into bed." She put her cool fingers on my forehead. "I'll bring you some fruit juice and aspirin."

"No. I don't need anything."

"Are you sure?"

I nodded.

"Want me to fix your covers?"

"No."

She went to the door, looked at me for a moment. "Sure you're all right?"

I nodded and she left. I rolled over and closed my eyes. I fell asleep almost instantly and slept heavily, no dreams, and woke up in the morning to the buzz of my alarm clock.

I went downstairs and drank a glass of orange juice. James was sitting at the table, eating cornflakes from the box and reading a comic book. I heard my parents walking around in their bedroom. I didn't want to see either of them.

I left the house and was at school before anybody else. The janitor had just unlocked the front door. I hung around in the halls till my homeroom teacher opened up our classroom. " 'Morning, Marylee," Mr. Hammar said, "you're here nice and early."

I opened my notebook and stared at a blank page. I looked down at my watch—the watch my mother had given me. I pulled it off—I couldn't bear to wear it now. Before I went to my first class I dropped it into my locker. The day passed queerly. Long stretches of time, minutes, even hours, disappeared, and I only knew they'd gone because the bell was ringing, or people were shifting to watch slides, or I found myself walking slowly to another class. At the end of the day I was the last one left in homeroom. I didn't want to go home. Mr. Hammar was ready to lock up. "Marylee, first one in and last one out," he said.

I gathered up my books and walked through the dim, quiet halls toward my locker. As I rounded the corner and approached the long flat line of metal lockers I saw a girl in a brown car coat trying first one locker, then another, lifting the handles and letting them fall. The last locker was mine. She opened it, stooped down, and picked up something. Then she saw me. She had my wristwatch in her hand. She was stealing my wristwatch. With a feeling of disbelief I saw her shove the watch into her pocket and walk away.

She was stealing from me. Stealing my watch, and I was letting it happen. She glanced back, saw me still standing there and gave me a sort of half-salute with her head. *Well*, she seemed to be saying, *what are you going to do about it?*

A sly, superior smile flitted across her face as if she

recognized me, knew that stealing from me was okay. Knew that I'd never say anything. I was the sort of person anyone could steal from. Her smile said it all— anyone could take anything from me, and I wouldn't say a word.

"Wait," I said. I swallowed. My throat was so dry. It was the first word I'd said in hours. "Wait!" I dropped my books with a thud. As if that were a signal, the girl in the brown coat started running. And I ran after her.

"Wait!" I screamed in a terrible explosion of pain and fury. "Do you hear me? This can't go on."

She was gone, though. I ran all the way down the stairs, but she was nowhere in sight. She'd run away, been scared off by me. On the landing I found my wristwatch. She must have panicked, and thrown it away. I was so surprised. It was crazy, but I felt absolutely elated. I'd done it. I'd opened my mouth, filled my lungs with air, and yelled as loud as I could. And stopped her from stealing my watch. Me, the coward.

I got my books and started home. It was still snowing, gray, clouded, damp. I walked fast. I was thinking about my mother, my father, James, me. Our family. It wasn't going to be the same again. No use pretending. Some things changed whether you wanted them to or not. I couldn't make my mother stop seeing that man. Couldn't make her start loving my father again. Couldn't control her life. But my own life was something else. I stopped, packed snow into a ball, and threw it at a big red STOP sign on the corner. My aim was perfect. The snow splattered right on the T.

Mimi the Fish

(From Mimi Holtzer's diary: *March 8, Who are you, Mimi, what are you, why are you here, what does it mean to be alive? Can fish tell other fish apart? Do parents always know their children? Do children always know their parents?*)

Mimi, phosphorescent, swam up through a murky sea. "Interesting! I'm a fish," she said. Her little light shone bravely. She swam with wings, pushing toward the surface. Light broke through the water in long rectangles. "Here I come," Mimi called. "I'm coming, you know!" Then she found it hard to breathe and woke, gulping for air. The quilt was over her head in bunches and folds. She punched her way free.

"A party, indeed," she muttered, remembering at once her mother saying the night before, "Mimi, honeypie, you never have your friends over here, only that gawky

77

Susan, why don't you have a party for all the boys and girls you know?"

"What all boys and girls?" Mimi had said.

"Why, Susan, of course, and—oh, Ruth Ann Levinson? Her mother is a customer. And boys, too, there must be a boy you like?" Mimi's mother waited, but Mimi said nothing. Only she and Susan knew how Mimi felt about Robert Rovere. Had her mother mentioned his name, Mimi would have managed an astonished lift of her eyebrows, a blank smile. Robert Rovere? Rō-ber Rō-vere? Who he?

"I was crazy about boys at your age, and they were crazy about me, too." Her mother touched the little yellow bow (to match her yellow sweater) perched in her nest of curled black hair. "I always used to have parties on Friday nights for all my friends, and after they left my mother and I would clean up together and talk everything over." Mimi's mother had smiled hopefully. "You could invite whomever you want. Daddy and I would stay in our room, quiet as mice. You can buy Cokes and chips, invite as many as you want. The more the merrier! You know your friends better than I do."

So she did. One good friend. Susan Gaspay. Mimi was no social butterfly, no life of the party, no with-it girl with a big gang of friends.

Besides, what kind of party could they have in the space behind the butcher shop that served as living room, dining room, and kitchen for Mimi's family? There was barely space enough for the four of them, although the room was large. But within its four walls, painted the same glaring, varnished-looking yellowish brown as the other rooms, were crowded two refrigerators, stove, sink, kitchen table, chairs, TV with a sagging green plush chair in front of it, a couch where newspapers, scarves, socks, and lunchbags accumulated, a glassed-in cabinet for dishes and silver, a sewing machine, and a washer and dryer.

"No party," she told her mother. "No."

In her room now, in the narrow windowless darkness, the radiator hissed. Was it morning? Or was it still night? Yawning, Mimi groped for the little white plastic clock on the floor. As she found it, the alarm went off in her hand.

In the kitchen, Mimi's mother was dressed for the butcher shop in a red sweater, the sleeves rolled up over the elbows. She wore a red bow in her hair, and two bright spots of rouge on her cheeks.

"Hello, honeypie, good morning," she said to Mimi, stuffing a load of washing into the machine. "There's cereal for you, bacon, milk, and buttered toast. How's the bacon, Gary?"

Gary, sitting at the table in his bathrobe, grunted something and stuck his nose into his milk, sucking it up with noises that reminded Mimi of bathroom plungers.

"I'm not very hungry," Mimi said.

"Put butter, sugar, and cream on the cereal, and it'll taste delicious. Your brother," she added, as if she were recounting one of his many virtues, "ate a big bowlful."

79

"I don't have an appetite yet," Mimi said. "Could I just drink some orange juice and have toast?"

"Absolutely not, missy. A good breakfast—"

"Eileen." From the butcher shop, Mimi's father called her mother.

"Coming right away, honeypie," her mother answered in a trilling voice. Then to Mimi, "A good breakfast is essential for health. Clean up everything in front of you. You can't expect to grow if you don't eat! Sometimes I look at you and marvel, where did I get such a thin daughter? You're like a drink of water, there's nothing to you. You're not like anyone else in the family."

Mimi nodded, looking at her bony knees showing beneath the hem of her nightgown. Bony elbows, bony hands, even her feet were bony. Birdbones, her mother called her. Her parents and her brother were all large people, tall, big-boned, heavy-fleshed, their skins shining as if oiled, perhaps from all the meat and butter and cheese and eggs they ate.

A fly hovered over the butter in its pink plastic bowl. Then it lit on the mouth of the red plastic milk container. Mimi sat on the edge of her chair, and an edge of her dream came back to her, for an instant. To swim away! Up and out of this greasy golden air.

There was a knock on the door connecting apartment and butcher shop. "Eileen!"

"Coming! It's raining, he's feeling grumpy today," Mimi's mother said confidentially. She opened the door to the butcher shop, then turned to say in a hasty half-whisper, "Eat!"

Mimi the Fish

Mimi swallowed a spoonful of oatmeal. "All right. All right. Go on. He's waiting for you."

Mimi's father was the butcher, her mother worked behind the counter in the shop. She greeted each customer by name, like an old friend. When she was a little girl, Mimi had thought these women, of whom her mother often spoke in intimate terms, really *were* her friends. While Mimi's father went into the icebox to take the meat off the hook her mother joked about the weather. If it was winter and sleeting outside, she'd say, "Now isn't that gorgeous weather. Suntan weather!" And if it was a miserable muggy summer day, the ceiling fan sluggishly stirring the hot air, she'd say, "A fine day, isn't it, so cool and fresh?" And the customer, Mrs. Grunbacher, or young Mrs. Levinson, or Mrs. Knoblock, or high-voiced Milly Tea—whoever it was—would laugh and say, "Eileen, you're too much!" By then, Mimi's father would be cutting the meat, out on the block where the customer could see that it was being properly trimmed. He would weigh the chops and Mimi's mother would wrap the meat in pink butcher paper and take the money, still making little jokes.

"When people smile, they don't mind the high prices so much," Mimi's mother said. "They don't blame us, they see we're all the same, we have to live just the way they do."

In the shop, every day, six days a week, Mimi's mother was cheerful. Even if she had a headache, she would still make her little jokes about the weather. But in the apartment, in the rooms behind the butcher shop, Mimi's mother seemed to fade. She scrubbed the two spots of color off her cheeks and wore a faded housecoat that reached just below her knees. Her voice, too, seemed to fade; when she wanted Mimi to do something she would start off cheerfully, as if Mimi were a customer, but if Mimi were feeling stubborn and argued with her mother, her mother's voice would quickly lose its bright timbre and cheer, and an aggravated tone would creep in.

"The bathroom needs cleaning," her mother might announce cheerfully. "And isn't this a beautiful day to clean it."

"You should make Gary clean the tub, he's the one who always leaves it dirty."

"Gary's just a little boy, honeypie."

"Good Lord! Little! He's bigger than me."

"You know what I mean, he's only nine years old—"

"He's strong and he's healthy as a horse. Why don't you ask him to do the work?"

"Boys are different. Anyway, he doesn't do a good job like you. You're so neat—"

"You mean if I start being a slob, I can get out of things like Gary?"

This might go on for five or ten minutes, until her mother said, "Mimi, you do what I say. Do you want me to call your father?" Her mother's skin glistened as if freshly smeared with oil. "I don't ask you to do that much," her mother always said, but in fact Mimi's mother wanted many things from her. She wanted Mimi to work in the butcher shop on Saturdays, to watch Gary after school, to clean the apartment, to be more open and cheerful, to get good marks but not to be too smart, to help Gary with his homework, to bring friends home, to eat everything on her plate, to grow taller and fatter, and to smile at her father.

Her father had heavy white hairless arms and big heavy hands, raw-looking, like fresh meat. He rarely spoke. If an argument between Mimi and her mother or Mimi and her brother went on too long, if the voices rose beyond a certain threshold known only to him, he would bang on the door between the shop and the house, or heave himself up from his plush chair and boot Mimi in the rear end.

Whenever her father rose like that Mimi wrote in her diary, "Kicked." Coming on the single word sometimes when she flipped through the pages, it appeared to her mysterious, terrifying, poisonous. Kicked. A word like a steel spring. In the same room with her father, even on peaceful evenings, she sometimes felt as if she were suffocating.

When she left the apartment that morning, it had stopped raining. Coming from those windowless rooms, Mimi stepped into the wet shining world as if she were plunging into a lake. She was sorry the rain was over. There was nothing so wonderful as spring rain. She could walk for hours in a warm rain.

Mimi greedily sniffed the air. The city had the harsh clean look of early spring. Oh, I love wet days! I love spring, I love life! Mimi thought fervently. I love Robert

Rovere! Then turning the corner she suddenly saw him ahead of her, walking with several other boys. At once, Mimi slowed down. Her cheeks became hot and moist.

She didn't dare catch up to Robert and pass him. She was afraid he would look at her and *know* how she felt about him. But the truth was he never looked at her. They had two classes together every day, but she might as well have been a piece of furniture, a desk, or a map stand, for all that he ever noticed her.

He was exceptionally good-looking. He was tall, slender, carried himself well, and every day wore a fresh crew-neck sweater in the softest wool. He had brown eyes flecked with amber and covered by long dark lashes that gave his face a rather tender look. Several girls were in love with him. However, there were things about Robert that disturbed Mimi: he was always combing his hair; he was not above mocking Miss Grey. Most of the other boys did the same. But Mimi wanted Robert to be perfect.

Only a few days before, a boy passing in the corridor had rapped on the door, shouted out "Hey, hey, Nellie Grey, your father says you may!"

Laughter rocked the class. Nellie was short, round, and gray as her name, gray as a dustball. She darted to the door on tiny bird feet encased in little gray shoes. "You! You there! Come back." Behind her back Robert stood and silently mimicked her futile gestures. His performance had been well received. Laughter and whistles.

Miss Grey came back to her desk. The pockets of flesh on her face were mottled with tiny red veins. Mimi's neck had been damp with pity; she wanted to hate Robert, but found it impossible. Instead, she despised herself. She had sat there and laughed, too, hadn't she?

In school she met Susan at the lockers. "I walked behind him all the way," she said at once.

They never said Robert's name. "Did he see you?"

"I don't think so."

"Too bad!"

"Are you kidding? If he'd seen me——" Mimi shuddered violently. "I was trapped! I couldn't get past him and those others—Benjie, Paul, and what's-his-face that's always following RR around. I just had to keep walking behind him." She told Susan about her mother's suggestion for a party. "She was really pushing it. I told her no."

"Why? It sounds like a good idea."

"Whose side are you on?"

"Yours. It still sounds like a good idea."

"Terrific. Who would I invite. You?"

"Oh, there are other kids." Susan was always calm. She was a tall blond girl with a large nose and a creamy complexion. She and Mimi had been friends for about a year.

"Think what you're saying, Susan. Think! Can you imagine my father staying put in his bedroom? Like a little *mouse*?"

"I am thinking," Susan said. "A kitchen party, you could make popcorn, we could fix things up, decorate, I mean. It might be fun. And you could invite *him*. It would be a way to get to know him."

"You're crazy. He'd refuse. Why would he come to a party at my house?"

"I hear he likes parties."

"Make-out parties, probably."

Susan plucked at her lower lip. "I have a plan. We'll find out first how he feels about you. Then, we can decide about the party."

"Find out how he feels about me! How do we do that?"

"Ask him," Susan said, sensibly.

"Ask him! Ask him what? Are you crazy, Susan? What do I do, go up to him and say, 'By the way, how do you feel about me? Oh, you don't even know who I am? I'm Mimi Holtzer. Now, how do you feel about me?' Terrific plan."

"Temper, temper," Susan said. "I'll think of something, you know me. Anyway, he knows who you are. He knows. He's been watching you. I saw him watching you yesterday in Nellie's class."

"You're making it up. You're saying that to make me feel good."

"I wouldn't do that. Would you make up things to tell me?"

"Of course not."

"Well, neither would I."

They stopped at the door to the science lab. Mimi tried to remember the day before in Nellie Grey's algebra class. What had she been thinking about? How had she been sitting? A conviction seized her that she had been chewing on her thumbnail, an unconscious habit which her mother said made her look like a rabbit. Had Robert really been watching her?

The bell rang. "Come on, girls, come on," Mr. Bradford called impatiently. "Inside!"

"Leave it to me," Susan said as they hurried toward their seats. "I'll take care of it."

"Susan, don't do anything. Nothing!"

"Girls—please!"

Mimi dropped into her seat. She tried to shake her head violently at Susan without attracting Mr. Bradford's attention.

Susan looked pointedly toward Robert, who sat two seats across from her, then pantomimed writing him a note. Again Mimi shook her head. No! Susan winked at her; her wink said, Relax, I'll take care of it.

Mr. Bradford asked if someone could define igneous rock. Susan folded a piece of paper and passed it to Robert. Volcanoes erupted in Mimi's mind: millions of years flashed by in a second. Robert was opening the note. Mimi thought of Nellie Grey's tenuous grasp on her dignity, of her mother's fat, shaven white legs, and then of her own hopeless passion for Robert Rovere. Did anything make sense? Her neck was sweating.

It wasn't till the end of the day that Susan had an answer from Robert. "Give it to me." Mimi held out her hand.

"You know, it was really a stupid idea to write that note," Susan said. "One of my lesser genius ideas. In fact, a real dumdum idea." She folded the note over three times.

"He hates me," Mimi said. "He wrote that he hates me."

"No, no. No, really. No, he didn't say that. But why don't I just tear it up, anyway."

"It's awful, I know it's craven of me, but I want to see it. You wrote it, and he answered it, and now I want to see it."

"Don't be stubborn."

"Give me the note, Susan."

"Listen, it's nothing. Really, it's nothing. Zero. Total nothing. If you don't see it, you won't miss a thing."

"I want to see it. Anyway."

Susan folded the note again so that it was very small and thick. "Come on, Mimi. Forget it, okay? Look, you're going to embarrass me, because it was my dum-dum idea, and—"

"Give—me—the—note," Mimi said. Bugles sounded. Drums rolled. She stood straight-backed, blindfolded, about to be shot through the eyes. She tore away the blindfold. *I will face my death like a woman*, she shouted. "I want to see it, Susan," she said. "You have to give it to me."

"It's your funeral," Susan sighed, handing Mimi the wad of notepaper.

Susan had written, "Robert, someone with the initials MH likes you very much. How do you feel about her? Respondez si'l vous pleeze on the other side."

Mimi turned over the paper. In a cramped scrawl, Robert had answered, "Tell her to go pluck a duck."

"It's not that bad," Susan said.

88

"It's terrible." Mimi crumpled the note and stuck it in her pocket.

"He didn't say he hated you. He just said—"

"I know what he said." Mimi walked out of the building followed by Susan. "He hates me."

"I'm sorry," Susan said. "It was my dumdum idea."

"All right! You said that enough times already." She took out the note and read it again. It hurt even more on the second reading. He could have said he didn't know her, or was interested in another girl, or not answered at all. She felt dumbly miserable. What had ever made her think even for one insane moment that Robert Rovere, splendid, beautiful RR, would be, could be even remotely interested in Mimi Holtzer, plain, skinny, drink-of-water Mimi?

"Forget him," she advised herself in her diary. "He's not worth the misery. He's crude, without feeling, insensitive. Never think about him again! Wipe him out completely from your mind!"

But she couldn't do it. All weekend, in fact, as she went about her chores in the house and the shop, she compulsively made up scenes in which (a) Robert followed her into Lincoln Park to confess he was and always had been madly, helplessly in love with her; (b) he was overheard telling another boy that Mimi Holtzer was far, far too good for the likes of him; (c) he implored her to believe the note was a hideous mistake, and begged her to wear his blue shetland wool sweater as a sign of forgiveness; and (d) barging into her house, he passionately declared he couldn't sleep, he couldn't eat, he could only think of her. In turn, Mimi was (a) sweetly understanding; (b) aghast at the poor boy's crumpled pride; (c) warm and forgiving; and (d) warm and understanding.

Monday, and the rest of the week, Robert stared at her all through science and algebra. Mimi never looked directly at him, but she knew he was staring. Once, in the hall, he seemed about to say something, but she veered away abruptly. She was afraid he would do something horrible. The worst part of the whole humiliating business was that she was still knocked out by him; her stomach knotted every time she walked into a classroom and saw him sitting there, beautiful and perfect.

After school on Friday, she was home, peeling potatoes, when her mother called from the butcher shop for Mimi to pick up the extension phone in the kitchen.

"Mimi? This is Robert. Do you want to go to the dance at the Y tonight?"

"Who?"

"Robert."

"Oh." She felt dazed and, picking up a pencil, scribbled the word "who" on the wall, then began to shade it in carefully.

"Robert *Rovere*," he said.

"Yes. I know." Her heart seemed to be beating in her ear (she was sure he could hear it), the ear to which she held the phone, the ear through which Robert Rovere's voice, smooth as salad oil, was sliding down to her thundering heart.

"Well?" he said.

"What?"

"The dance," he said.

"Oh! Okay."

"Okay about the dance?"

"Yes. Okay."

"Well," he said, "then do you want me to meet you at the Y, or come to your house?"

She tried to remember exactly where the Y was. She wrote "Y" on the wall in a block letter. There was a long silence. She was still trying to remember where the Y was. She had only known its location all her life.

"You there?" he said.

"Yes!"

"I'll come to your house."

"Okay." How many times had she said okay? Couldn't she say anything else? "Good-bye," she said, hastily. "Oh! Wait! Robert. Robert Rovere! Do you know where I live?" Why had she said his name that way? She wanted to punch her head against the wall.

"Broad Street," he said.

"Near the elementary school," she said. "Come around to the back. Okay?" She'd said it again. "Thank you." She hung up the phone. At once she was convinced the entire call was a practical joke. And she, the fool, had even said, Thank you!

Her mother came into the kitchen. "Who was that?"

"A boy. I'm going to the Y tonight, to a dance." The last words came out in a mumble. Was she?

"You're going out with a boy? To a dance? Well, that's wonderful, honeypie."

"Yes."

"Get dressed up, you're going to change your clothes, aren't you? Who's the boy?"

"Robert Rovere." Her lips hardly seemed to want to part to say the name.

"Robert Rovere!" her mother repeated in thrilled tones, as if she knew Robert and were as infatuated as Mimi.

Mimi stared at her. "I've got to finish peeling the potatoes," she said, going back to the sink.

She was sure it was a hoax. Why would Robert Rovere ask her to a dance? It didn't make sense. He hated her. It had sounded like him—sort of. It could have been one of his friends, impersonating him. She called up Susan. "Susan? Listen! Would Robert Rovere do a mean thing like calling me, asking me to go out, and then not show up?"

"I don't know," Susan said.

"Do you think it was really *him*?"

"I don't know. What do you think?"

"I don't *know*," Mimi said, laughing half hysterically. "I don't really know anything about him."

"Oh, God," Susan moaned. "I'll keep my fingers crossed for you."

All through supper, Mimi veered wildly between belief and disbelief. He was coming. He wasn't coming. It had been him on the phone. It had been a practical joke. She decided not to do anything, not change clothes, not wash her face. Nothing. But her mother wouldn't leave her alone. She kept popping out of the butcher shop to ask if Mimi had changed yet. Finally, Mimi put on a fresh blouse, combed her hair and cleaned her fingernails. At the last moment she cleaned her ears, too. Every time she looked at the clock, she felt sick in the pit of her stomach. Fool! Fool!

There was a knock at the back door. "You get it," Gary said. He was eating a chocolate bar and reading a comic.

Robert was standing among the coats and boots in the dark shed, frowning into the light of the kitchen. "Hello," Mimi said. Her eyes felt damp, and strange. "You called me this afternoon?"

"Sure," he said.

"You did!" She stared at him. How perfectly beautiful he was. His hair was freshly combed, he wore a sweater she hadn't seen before, a deep forest green with a vee neck. She felt humble before such beauty. "Come in." She was astonished to hear that she sounded normal. She put on her jacket and opened the connecting door to the butcher shop. "I'm going."

"You're going?" her mother said. "Wait. Wait a minute." She was washing the inside of one of the glass cases. "Bring him in."

"What?"

"Bring him in to meet us, meet your father."

"Mom!" Mimi exclaimed. "No-ooo." She closed the door hastily. "I'm ready," she said to Robert. " 'Bye, Gary," she called over her shoulder, leading the way out through the shed.

Outside there was a thin moon rising in the still-light sky. Robert smiled at her. Suddenly she felt wonderful, capable of anything. He was here! He had come to take her to a dance! Robert Rovere! She rose on her toes, almost dancing over the gravel driveway.

"Mimi!" Her mother came running out of the house after them, holding a package wrapped in white paper. "Hel*lo*," she said to Robert. "My daughter didn't even introduce you! Some manners. I'm Mimi's mother."

"Hello, Mrs. Holtzer. I'm pleased to meet you."

"*What* a beautiful night for dancing," Mimi's mother said. "Do you do all the new dances, Robert?"

Robert smiled politely. "I try to."

"I like to dance, too, I love to dance. I try to keep up with things. Ask Mimi. Don't I, Mimi? Don't I dance right in our kitchen sometimes?" She laughed girlishly.

"Yes, you do." Stepping back, Mimi made frantic signs to her mother. "Mom, we're late. We have to *go*."

"Oh, I can take a hint, a very subtle hint," Mimi's mother held up two fingers. "Two's company, and three's a crowd. Right, Robert?" She put the white package into Mimi's hands. "Limburger cheese for Milly Tea, Mimi. We got a case of imported Limburger in today, Robert. Straight from Belgium. We get it only for our special customers. Mimi, I promised Milly you'd deliver it tonight."

"Tonight!" Mimi echoed. "We're not going that way."

"You'll be going right by her place."

"Why don't you send Gary?" But Mimi knew her mother never asked Gary to do anything.

"Milly's crazy about Limburger," her mother said to Robert. "I don't know why, I can't get past the smell, myself."

"I'll do it tomorrow," Mimi said, trying to hand back the package of cheese which was already beginning to broadcast its strong odor.

Her mother shook her head. "I promised her, Mimi. I just talked to her on the phone. She's having company and she's expecting the cheese. You don't mind, do you, Robert? A little errand like this?"

"That's fine, Mrs. Holtzer."

Mimi's mother gave Robert's arm an admiring little squeeze. "You're a sweetheart. Well, good-bye. Mimi, wake me up when you get home. Now you two, have a barrel of fun for yourselves. Wish I was going with you, but I have to get back to work. The master calls." She laughed. "No rest for the wicked." She went past them, around the side of the building.

Mimi stared down at the package in her hands, feeling a familiar frustration. Then she took a deep breath. She wasn't going to let her mother spoil her evening. "Ready?" she said to Robert. The sooner she got rid of the cheese the better.

"Who's Milly Tea?" Robert said as they started out.

"Milly Thomas. A lady who's sort of a friend of my mother's. She comes into the shop all the time."

"Oh, T like the letter, not golf tees."

Mimi shook her head. "Tea like tea you drink. Milly went to England on a tour once, and now she only drinks tea."

"Bloody smashing," Robert said. "Drinks tea and eats Limburger."

"That's the idea. She's really a nice lady."

"Little weird, eh?"

"I guess so." Mimi shifted the package to her other hand. The air was cool and quiet. A few cars passed. It was not yet quite dark. Mimi tried to forget the cheese and her mother and concentrate on being with Robert. Here I am, she said to herself, going to a dance with *Robert Rovere.* It's really happening. She glanced up at him. His profile was pure and clean. For the first time she noticed that he had the faintest beginnings of a mustache.

"That cheese smells," he said.

"I know. I'm sorry." She held the cheese in the hand farthest from him, but the smell seemed to be creeping up her arm. "Anyway, it's not a cheap-o smell," she said. "This stuff costs like the moon." They turned onto Montcalm Street. Milly lived in an attic apartment of a large red house.

"What's the number?" Robert said.

"Number?"

"The house number," he said distinctly. His voice was controlled.

"I don't know, but I know the house when I see it. It has a big porch and a red door. Oh, here it is." Mimi ran up the steps and rang the bell. "I'll just be a second," she called. She heard Milly coming down the stairs. Hurry up, hurry up. She wanted to get rid of the lump of cheese and get back to Robert. They were still a little stiff and strange together.

"My mother sent this—" she began as the door was opened, but instead of Milly, a chubby boy who looked a little bit like Gary stood there.

"Hello, where's Milly? I have the Limburger for her." She tried to hand him the cheese.

"Phew!" He screwed up his face. "That stinks. There's no Milly here. You've got the wrong house." He slammed the door.

"Hey," Mimi called. She put her finger on the bell, then noticed that the little printed name tag under the bell wasn't Thomas. She *had* come to the wrong house. Oh, how stupid, how embarrassing. She dropped the cheese into her pocket and rejoined Robert.

"What happened?" he asked.

"Wrong house. I don't know how I did that. I was so sure she lived there." For a moment she walked backward, staring at the house with the red door. She could have *sworn* that was the one. None of the other houses on that block, or on the next block, either, looked like Milly's.

Mimi put her hand over the cheese in her pocket, hoping to muffle the odor. If she had her way, she'd throw the damn stinking stuff straight into the nearest sewer. But she didn't dare. The cheese *was* expensive. Her mother would have purple fits. She hated to admit it, but the cheese would have to go to the dance with her. Either that, or walk all the way back to her house.

She bit her lip. No way. She didn't dare ask Robert that, after already asking him to go out of his way to Montcalm Street. He was probably already regretting that phone call. Must have done it on the spur of the moment, she thought gloomily. Curious about her. Well, now he knew.

Her first date ever, her first date with *RR*, and she was botching it up, stuck toting around a large dumb messy package of cheese that, moment by moment, smelled more and more like somebody's dirty feet. If only her mother had listened to her in the first place, Mimi thought furiously, and let her deliver it tomorrow, instead of always insisting on having her own way. She was always butting in, making suggestions, and shoving things on Mimi. Never left her alone.

"Well, what do we do now?" Robert said, sticking his hands in his back pockets in the manner of a man who is learning patience.

"Well—on to the dance, I guess." She was so embarrassed she couldn't think of a thing to say, and they walked the rest of the way in a silence as thick as the odor of the cheese.

As they climbed the steps of the Y, Mimi made hasty plans. She wiped her hands surreptitiously on the sides of her jacket. Get rid of her coat, go to the bathroom, wash her hands of the cheesy stink, come back to Robert and—well, *sparkle*.

Inside, the Y was well lit and too warm. Kids were streaming in for the dance. "Hi!" "Oh, hi ya!" Robert seemed to know everybody. Girls kept passing, giving him little playful shoves.

"Hi, Robbie."

"Roberto!"

"Big R, hel-lol"

There was a mob around the snack bar, and not an empty inch on the coatrack outside the dance hall. A man standing at the door wearing a little red bow tie was yelling over the noise, "You latecomers, just hang on to your coats, just wear them to dance in. You latecomers, just hang on to your coats—"

"Where's the girls' room?" Mimi said, or rather, screamed over the noise of the band. It was a local group, Mother Carey and Her Chickens, two guitarists, a drummer, and a singer.

"No place to hang our coats," Robert said, apparently misunderstanding.

Oh, *no*, Mimi thought. She didn't want to ask again for the bathroom. Her neck was hot and damp. She could smell the cheese as if it were being held under her nose. Maybe no one else noticed. Maybe the cheese smell was blending in with all the other smells. The snack bar was selling hot dogs, Cokes, potato chips. The air was full of grease and the perfumed smells rising from the crowd.

"Want to dance?"

"Sure!" Mimi screamed over the hard, loud exciting sound of Mother Carey and Her Chickens. They squeezed onto the dance floor. So close to him, Mimi noticed that Robert smelled of something sweet, like lily of the valley. *She* smelled of Limburger cheese. The room was packed with kids dancing, shouting to each other, watching the dancers and each other. There was constant movement of people off and on the floor, in and out of the room, to and from the snack bar.

"Come on, baby, baby," Mother Carey, the singer, pleaded, shaking her hips energetically, "baby, come on, baby baby mine, baby, you and me gonna show the world what we can do, do do do, do do do, baby, oooooh, ba-aaa-aaa-beeee. . . ."

Mimi threw herself into the dance, the music, the beat. But whenever she looked at Robert, his eyes were closed as he danced, or he was looking somewhere else. Look at me, she willed him, look at me. But he didn't. Probably trying to forget her, the smelly lady from the butcher shop. . . .

"Let's get a drink," he said. They pushed through the crowd to the snack bar. Mimi kept her lips frozen in a happy smile so that if Robert did happen to look at her he would know she was having a super time. In her pocket the awful package of cheese bumped against her side.

They made a little space for themselves, holding cans of soda up to their mouths. Kids were screaming to each other. Someone trampled on Mimi's feet. The floor was littered with crackling, empty chips bags. In the other room the music began again.

Robert stared over Mimi's head. Bored, she thought desperately. Bored silly with her. Well, the evening was a disaster. Total disaster. Really wrecked. Thanks to her mother. Mimi's hands curled around the soda can, she puffed despairingly. She couldn't think of one thing to say, nothing on her mind but cheese, stinking smelly cheese.

Come *on*, Mimi, there's more to you than Limburger cheese. Say something. Anything! All the times she and Susan had mapped out sparkling, witty conversations. Never mind that old advice about getting the boy to talk about himself. That was too down on girls. Instead, they'd decided that nothing worked like sincerity. So, Mimi? Be sincere.

What if she told him she sometimes dreamed of being a fish, gliding free, her hair streaming back, half-fish, half-girl. No, she could never tell him that. The way he'd mocked Nellie Grey.

Several people glanced strangely at her. She was hot, sweating. The odor rising from her jacket was growing stronger by the moment. She tried planning how she would tell Susan about all this. . . . *It was really funny, I felt like I was turning into a lump of Limburger myself. Only he didn't think it was funny. What can you expect? No sense of humor. Blah.* . . . Only her heart wasn't in it. She thought a little crazily of emptying her Coke over her head, or better still, straight into her pocket to drown the cheese.

They drank another soda. "Do you fight with your folks?" she said, desperate to break the silence.

"Not much. Do you?"

"Some," she said gloomily.

"It's just my mother and me," Robert said. "My father's dead."

"Oh! I'm sorry."

"Don't be. I never knew him."

"Oh," she said again. It was one of those conversations that couldn't get off the ground. She was practically grateful when a large redheaded boy who went to one of the parochial schools stopped to talk to Robert about the Minolta his father had bought him for Christmas. "I'm taking some fantastic pictures, man," the boy said, glancing sideways at Mimi. "I'm a great photographer." He smiled modestly, then screwed up his nose. "Who took off their shoes here, man?"

Mimi's heart sank.

"What's the matter?" Robert said, glancing blandly around.

"Something *stinks*."

Here it comes, Mimi thought. She couldn't look at Robert. In a moment he would point at her and say, *She does. Mimi Holtzer stinks!*

"I don't smell anything," Robert said. "You, Mimi?"

For a moment she thought she'd heard wrong. Robert was smiling conspiratorially at her. She stared at him in utter astonishment. "No, I don't smell anything," she managed to say faintly.

"I smell something putrid, man," the redhead insisted. "Like something's dead in here."

"Must be your imagination," Robert said. "Listen, I

heard this funny story I want to tell you. There was this kid who didn't know the answer to a question and—"

Mimi burst out laughing.

"Wait a second, hold on," Robert said. But Mimi couldn't stop laughing. How about that! Robert was sticking up for her. It was too wonderful. The cheese had suddenly become their secret.

"Check the bottom of your shoes," the redhead said. "I think you stepped in something, Rovere."

"He's obsessed," Robert said to Mimi.

"Poor boy," she agreed, shaking her head sadly. "Must have a nose problem." She looked at him innocently. "Do you always smell things?" Robert choked on his Coke and Mimi pounded him on the back.

When they left the Y later, the streets were quiet. They hummed one of the songs they'd danced to. At her house, in the front window of the darkened butcher shop, three meat hooks gleamed. Mimi and Robert walked, hand in hand, around the side of the building, gravel crunching underfoot. The moon was high now, sliced thin, riding like a cheerful boat above them.

"I'm sorry about the cheese," she said.

"Cheese? What cheese?" he said, and kissed her. She hadn't known that kissing and laughing together could be so delightful. Robert's lips tasted sweet, like Coke. They staggered together, laughing, into the dark shed. A box fell over. "Shh!" Mimi wound her arms around his neck and kissed him back. "Thanks, I had a wonderful time. Good night!"

She opened the kitchen door quietly. The house was

dark. The familiar smells of her family closed in on her. She took the cheese out of her pocket, fumbled quietly toward the table. Don't make any noise, she warned herself.

Wake me up, her mother had said, but Mimi wanted to be alone, to think about Robert, the surprising wonderful way things had changed. "*What* cheese?" she sang out suddenly, unable to keep still. Then clapped her hand over her mouth. But too late.

Her mother's door opened. "Mimi? That you?" The light snapped on. Her mother was wearing a frilly blue nightgown, but she didn't look as if she'd been asleep. "I was waiting for you," she confirmed. "I couldn't sleep a wink till you got home. How was it? Did you have fun? Did you have a wonderful time? I want to hear everything."

Mimi put the package of cheese on the table. "It was fine," she said.

"What did you do? Did you dance a lot? Did a lot of boys ask you to dance?"

"No. I danced just with Robert, and—that's all. Just danced."

"It must have been wonderful, he's such a good-looking boy." Her mother opened the refrigerator and took out milk and butter. "I'm going to make you toast and cocoa while we talk."

"I don't want anything to eat, Mom," Mimi said, moving toward her room.

"Just a cup of cocoa," her mother insisted. "You need it after dancing all night." She put the pan on the stove and measured in cocoa and sugar. "I bet you were popular, the most popular girl there," she said. "The prettiest girl in the room," she sang, stirring the milk.

She poured two cups of cocoa and sat down at the table, smiling. "Sit down, honeypie. Let's talk."

Reluctantly, Mimi sat down across from her.

"Did they decorate the room? We used to have balloons, crêpe-paper twists, even different colored lights for our dances."

"It was just at the Y, Mom."

"Were lots of kids there?"

"Tons of them. I couldn't even hang up my coat, had to wear it all evening, and the cheese—"

"The cheese?" her mother repeated, and just then noticed the Limburger in the middle of the table. "I *wondered* what smelled." Her nose wrinkled as she picked up the package. "This is the Limburger cheese? The cheese I gave you for Milly? What's it doing here?"

"I brought it home. I couldn't find Milly's house. I went to her house on Montcalm, I *thought* it was her house, but they said she didn't live there."

"But, Mimi, honeypie," her mother said, putting the cheese into one of the refrigerators, "I told you Milly Tea moved to Howlett Avenue."

"You didn't tell me that," Mimi said, stiffening.

"Why, yes, I did, honeypie. I'm sure I did," her mother said softly, in the same wheedling voice she used to ask Mimi to scrub the bathtub. "Howlett Avenue. I told you."

"You never did," Mimi said. Had her mother given her that stinking lump of Limburger on *purpose*? It was a very crazy thought. But Mimi remembered how her mother had come dashing out after her and Robert, so insistent Milly Tea *had* to have that cheese tonight. And now she didn't even seem to care that the cheese had never been delivered.

"You never told me about Milly Tea moving. I had to carry that cheese around all evening."

"All evening," her mother repeated in a small voice. "It must have been terrible."

"It was," Mimi said unsparingly. Sure, things had come out fine in the end. But no thanks to her mother. She pushed away the cocoa cup and went to her room. Her mother followed, apologizing.

"I ruined your evening. I can see it on your face, you're mad at me.

"Mom, I'm tired." She kicked off her shoes and sat tensely on the edge of her bed. That fine swimming feeling, that lightness was draining away. Why couldn't her mother leave her alone?

"The cheese in your coat pocket all evening," her mother lamented. "That *awful* smell—"

"It doesn't matter," Mimi said furiously. Okay, okay, maybe her mother hadn't done it maliciously. Had just *had* to see Robert and didn't care what excuse she used. So she'd come running out with that cheese. Had to live Mimi's life *every minute!*

Sitting down heavily next to Mimi, her mother put her arms around her. "Your first date," she mourned, "and I ruined it."

Mimi stiffened under the weight of her mother's moist

arms, suffocated by her mother's smells of meat and sweat.

"Mimi, I'm sorry! I wanted you to have a wonderful time on your first date. It only comes once, it should be perfect. I remember. Oh, I remember." Her mother rocked Mimi back and forth. She felt trapped, unable to struggle free of her mother's grasp. Let go of me, she wanted to scream. Let me go. *Let go.*

"Life goes so fast, Mimi," her mother said, rocking her. "Those wonderful days, I think of them now and I can't believe it was so long ago. First you're young and happy, and then suddenly you're grown up. And it's all different. You'll find out. You'll see."

Something wet fell on Mimi's face. She looked up, astonished. Her mother's eyes were shining with tears. "Oh, Mimi, I am sorry. I am so sorry." Her face wrinkled with tears. "I wanted so much," her mother cried, rocking Mimi back and forth.

It was terrible to hear her mother cry. Mimi thought of her mother behind the butcher counter, joking with the customers, or in the dim varnished kitchen, or in the narrow closed bedroom with her silent father. And she ached with a new dumb pain for her mother.

Her mother's tears fell on Mimi's cheeks. "Oh, Mimi," her mother said in a strangely agonized voice. "Oh, my Mimi." She patted Mimi's head heavily, clumsily, caressing her, yet at the same time pushing her head down in that loving, strangling embrace. And Mimi let her. Just for that moment, she gave up fighting. She bent her head, almost willingly. It was like a gift to her mother. She

could be generous. She was young. She could let her
mother hold her, dreaming of Mimi's life as her life.
Because even now, with her head bent, she was moving
away. She was moving away from her mother, out of this
life, these closed rooms, swimming free, swimming toward her own life, into her own blue sea. Swimming
strongly and freely away. Mimi the fish! Good-bye, she
sang in fish language. Good-bye, good-bye!

Dear Bill, Remember Me?

Dear Bill,

Well, guess who this is, writing to you after all these years! Four years, to be exact. Today is Sunday, October 5, and the last time I saw you was on a Saturday in May. May 7, to be exact. Four years, five months, and two days, to be ex—

Dear Bill,

Remember me? It's been a long time since I saw you last. I figure (roughly speaking) about four years. Mucho water under the dam, as the saying goes. I wonder if you would recognize me now. I bet you wouldn't call me Bitsy anymore, even though I'm still not the world's tallest woman. But I've changed quite a bit (Nature, old boy, Nature) and so have certain other people around here that you used to know.

My mother, for instance, has gotten plump! What

happened was, she decided to go back to work (driving a bus—cool, *n'est-ce pas?*) and give up smoking at the same time. But she still *wants* to smoke like crazy, so instead she eats every chance she gets. You should see the lunch bag she takes to work. Dad says everything except the kitchen sink goes into that bag. Dad is the same except he had to get glasses because he can't see little stuff like telephone numbers. And the other person you might be interested in hearing about, Judy—well, Judy is Judy. She's in college and, actually, I don't see that much of her anymore.

And what about you? Have you changed? I hope not. I always thought you were perfect, and I still th—

Dear Bill Old Chum,

This is Kathy speaking. Kathy Kalman. (Bitsy, to you.) Remember? Well, it's been a long time all right, Bill, plenty of water flowing under the dam, and thank goodness no one calls me Bitsy anymore. I never liked that name. Still, if we could have one of our good old long talks again, I wouldn't care what you called me—Kid, Bitsy, KK, Shorty—anything would be okay!

I've never been able to talk to anybody the way I talked to you. You listened to me, Bill. You took me seriously, me and my ideas, and even though you were so much older (seven years, remember?) you didn't look down on me, you didn't think it was beneath you to talk to me. You'd come over to see Judy, carrying a book under your arm and you'd be early, as usual (you

110

said it was a bad habit, that you had to get everywhere before everyone else), and if Judy wasn't ready, you'd say, "Come on, Bitsy, talk to me. Keep me company." Remember?

We'd go outside by the kitchen door and sit next to each other on top of the wooden steps leading from our back porch down to the yard, and we'd talk. Talk about *everything*. Sometimes, it would be about school. I told you once how Miss Fish, my gym teacher in fifth grade, had paddled one of the girls in front of everyone. Pulled down her pants in the shower room and paddled her over her knee. I said to you that if she ever tried to do that to me, I would kill her. You didn't laugh. You didn't say, Oh you know you don't mean that, the way people do all the time. You put your arm around me, and you nodded, and said you knew how I felt.

Another time, you asked me, "If nobody hears the tree fall in the forest, has it fallen?" At first, I didn't know what you meant. It sounded so funny. But you were serious. You said philosophers had thought about this for thousands of years. "My own version, Bitsy, is: If I sit in my room and no one knows I'm there, how can *I* be sure I'm there?"

"But you are there, Bill."

"How do you know, Bitsy? How do I know? How do I know that I'm real, that I truly exist? What if it's all a dream? What if you're in my dream now, and I'm only part of your dream? How can you be sure?"

I wanted to laugh. I couldn't understand it. (I think

I understand now.) You were always saying funny things, mocking things, mocking yourself, your nose especially.

Are you surprised how much I remember of things you said to me? ~~I remember other stuff, too, like the time you kis~~ I only wish I could remember everything, instead of just bits and pieces.

Well, Bill, reading back over this letter, I can see that I've really strayed off the beaten path, gone all around Robin Hood's barn, as my mother says. What I started out to say, what I wanted to write about was, Congrats, Old Chum, congrats. It's not every day a good old friend ups and—

Dear Bill,

Remember me? It's been one heck of a long—

Dear Bill,

Surprise! After all these years, you must be wondering why you're suddenly hearing from—

Dear Bill,

Just a brief note to say congratu—

Dear Bill,

All morning I've been trying to write you a letter and not getting very far. Every time I write something it sounds stupid to me and I give up. Do you remember me? Judy Kalman's ~~little~~ younger sister? I guess you remember Judy, all right. (Ha-ha.)

112

See what I mean about sounding stupid?!

The thing is, my head is full of stuff I want to tell you, and questions you haven't been around to answer for four years, and—

Look, I don't mean that as an accusation. Lots of people break their promises. I'm positive you had tons of other stuff on your mind. Anyway, if you want to be exact about it, I guess it wasn't actually a promise. I mean, you didn't say, *I promise* in so many words. You just said, "Bitsy, we'll keep in touch. Okay?" And I said, "Yes."

I can see now that I was really a dope to think that was a promise and to go on waiting for years to hear from you. I guess you'd laugh if you could have seen me jump when the phone rang, or run for the mail every day after I heard you went away to college. My mother used to say, "Who do you think is going to write you, Kathy?" And I'd say, "Oh—nobody." And she'd say, "That's what I thought, because you don't write anybody." But I would have written you, Bill, if I'd known where. Would you have written me back?

Dear Bill,

This is ridiculous. I've been trying to write you a letter all morning and not getting anywhere. Well, this is it. I'm just getting on with this, writing whatever comes into my head, and the heck with it!

One thing I've been dying to tell you is that we read *Cyrano* in English. And guess who it made me think of right away! I love Cyrano, Bill. I adore him. "A great nose indicates a great man—genial, courteous, intellectual, virile, courageous . . ." Cyrano de Bill!

All those jokes about your nose. You said your nose was so goddamned big it got in the way of your seeing straight. (It never occurred to me then that you might be self-conscious. Well, you shouldn't have been. Big nose or not, I thought you were terrific-looking.) You used to intone, *Who knows what evil lurks in this nose? The Nose knows.* You'd put on your Fiendish Murderer face. And remember Mr. P.R.O. Biz Kiss, the Inquiring Reporter? "Where my nose goes, I follow, sniffing out the truth wherever it may lead." Mr. P.R.O. Biz Kiss could flare his nostrils and twitch his nose like a rabbit at the same time. Very talented, he was!

Bill—remember the time I sneaked up on you and Judy? That was a kid-sister, bratty kind of thing to do. I always wanted to explain to you about that, because I felt you were disappointed in me. (Were you?) That day, I was coming home from school, thinking how strange things were. I don't know why it happened just then, but all of a sudden that day, I had a different view of everything. Cars looked weird to me, and the clothes people wore, sidewalks, houses. As if everything was unreal. I kept thinking, Where did all this come from? How did it all get here? I had a feeling that someone, maybe God, could just peel off our whole city from the face of the earth like some cruddy scab. I suppose, for the first time, I was really thinking about things the way you always did, not just accepting everything—here I am, here's my parents and Judy, here's our house, school, the stores, and here it belongs. Instead, I had this dizzy feeling of it all being—well, superficial, not really *rooted.*

It was spring, I remember, and the city maintenance crew had just come along and filled up the potholes in our street and suddenly it terrified me that beneath the smooth, seemingly solid road was just a lot of dirt. Everything was so flimsy, everything I'd ever thought of as solid and unmovable. Cars and trucks traveled over roads, and houses stood on foundations, but I felt that in a moment it could all crumple like paper.

And then I came to our house—we were living upstairs on Second Street then, but we've moved, did you know that?—and as I started up the stairs, I was testing every step because I still had that queer scary feeling of everything being impermanent. And suddenly I knew that you and Judy were in our living room, that you were all alone in the house, and that you were making love.

As soon as I thought that, I started creeping quietly up the stairs. I didn't know why, but thinking about you and Judy made me forget the other sickening, frightening thoughts I'd been having. I stopped feeling dizzy and went on quietly, as quietly as I could, up the stairs. I didn't know what I was going to do. I really and truly didn't know, didn't think to myself that I was doing something sneaky or wrong.

I just kept creeping up, opened the door as quietly

as I could, and walked quietly into the living room. And just as I'd somehow known I'd find you, you both were there, on the couch together.

Judy saw me first. "Get out!" she yelled. The two of you fell apart, sort of jumped up or scrambled off the couch. I couldn't move. I felt—I don't know how to say it—hurt, I guess. Isn't that stupid? I mean, I *knew* what I was going to see. I'd had sort of a pre-vision. And yet, I just felt so hurt, so bad.

"You little spy," Judy said. Her cheeks were all red, shiny, as if she had a fever. "Spy! Sneak!" I shook my head. I wanted to explain, to say something, but nothing would come out.

I could hear my heart, or feel it, I wasn't sure which, making this hollow sound inside me. I'd never heard it before and it scared me terribly. I thought, *I'm going to die right now. Because I did this.* And still, all I could do was stand there and shake my head. I think I was waiting for you to say something. It was like I was in a spell and only you could break it. You were looking at me, your blond hair sticking out every which way, and your eyes sad, I thought, because I'd done something to hurt you.

And then—isn't it funny, queer, I mean—then I can't remember what happened next. I don't remember leaving the room or anything like that. The next thing I remember is Judy following me around offering me money not to tell Mom. I hated her for that, for thinking I'd betray her or you. And I guess she hated me, figuring I was holding it over her head. But torture wouldn't have made me reveal one single tiny fraction of what I'd seen. (One day I locked myself in the bathroom, poked a needle into my thumb four times, one time for each letter of your name, and with each drop of blood swore myself to silence.)

Are you laughing your head off, Bill? I wouldn't blame you, but I hope not. I hope you can understand that I was eleven and you were eighteen and I thought you were very special. Once you said to me, "Bitsy, when you grow up, you're going to drive some guy crazy." That was the time you kissed me. I guess you hardly remember it, since it wasn't a real kiss. I mean, it wasn't on the mouth or anything. You kind of stroked my hair and then you kissed me on the cheek. And you said, "You better be sure and let me know when you're sixteen. I want to be there when that time comes."

Well, I'm fifteen and one-half now, Bill, almost there, but I guess it doesn't matter anymore. I mean, I read about you and Lucille Lacy Heller Marginy in the newspapers—

Dear Bill,

This is a letter from an old friend who will probably remain nameless, but who wants to speak frankly to you concerning the Marginy woman. 1. She is thirty years old. 2. She has been married before. 3. She has two kids who are both spoiled. I know this for a fact because ~~Randy Southworth~~ a trusted friend has been Mrs.

Marginy's baby-sitter twice when she couldn't get her regular sitter, and this friend could do nothing whatsoever with the children. 4. She is too old for—

Dear Bill,

It's been quite a few years since I saw you last. Over four years, since it was in May four years ago that you and my sister, Judy, broke up. I happened to be there at the time it happened. Do you remember?

We were all out riding in your car, your old jalopy you called Spirit of Syracuse. I think Judy was mad at you because you let me come along.

I kept wishing you'd say, "Bitsy, come on up in front with us." Over and over I imagined you saying, "Move over, Judy, make room for Bitsy." But I didn't say anything. I was conscious of trying not to butt in, not to make too much of a pest of myself. I was just glad to go anyplace with you and Judy. I never thought Judy was nice enough to you, and I told myself you only liked her because she was so pretty. (Mom and Dad have noticed that my CQ—clumsy quotient—goes up when Judy comes home and they've tried to straighten me out —or up—by telling me I have no need to be jealous just because Judy is prettier and basically more successful in school.) I'm not jealous, truly. I like who I am. I've liked who I am ever since I knew you, Bill, because you liked me. But that didn't stop me from having spiteful eleven-year-old thoughts about my sister.

I was telling myself my pretty sister looked like a

Talking Barbie and, sitting behind her, I decided I could see a short piece of cord sticking out of her back. Pull the cord and Talking Barbie says, "Hello! I am Talking Barbie. I am taking a ride with Talking Ken. Talking Ken and I are having fun. Talking Ken and I are going to swim. Watch me swim in my sexy bikini."

I got myself all wrapped up, concentrating really hard on that idea. Mind over matter. Maybe if I concentrated superhard I could really turn Judy into Talking Barbie and then you and I would pack her up and ship her back to the Barbie factory to find Malibu Barbie, Talking Francie, and Growing Barbie.

When I finally tuned in on you and Judy again, you were fighting. That kind of low-voice fighting, where people still sound polite, and you can't figure out what's going on. Judy was saying, "You're supersensitive, Bill, about being poor, I never meant it that way."

And you said, "Supersensitive, my ass!"

That was the end of the low voices. Judy said she wasn't putting up with talk like that. And you told her that was ridiculous. And she said you'd better stop calling her names. And you said she was being juvenile.

"Okay!" she said. "Okay. Stop the car! I want to get out."

You wouldn't stop. You said that was silly and immature, you weren't going to let her walk ten miles back to the city.

"That's my decision, not yours," Judy said.

And suddenly you stopped the car. And she got out. For about two seconds, I was joyful, waiting for you to drive off so I could leap over the back seat and sit next to you, right where Judy had been sitting. Then she remembered me. "Okay, Bitsy, out! We're walking!"

And we walked. You drove away. I was furious with her because it was a hot day, the road stunk of carbon monoxide fumes from the cars whizzing by, and besides all that, I was barefoot.

You doubled back for us. We'd been walking for about twenty minutes, and I was so relieved. But Judy was too proud to get into the car without an apology. You said you had nothing to apologize for and that she was acting even more ridiculous and immature than you had thought her capable of acting.

I think I remember all that, practically word for word, because I was really torn. I was rooting for you, and yet I couldn't help being on my sister's side, too, mad as I was at her. "Come on, Judy, let's get in the car," I said. You were leaning on the window, your arms crossed. You winked at me.

"Come on, Judy," you said, "listen to Bitsy."

"Forget it." Judy started walking again. "Forget it, forget it, just *forget* it," she said, passing right by you.

"I'll forget it, all right," you said. "I'll forget you. That won't be too hard!" And you drove away, then suddenly backed up, stuck your head out the window and called, "Bitsy, we'll keep in touch. Okay?"

I said, "Yes!" And then you were really gone.

I caught up with Judy. We walked along for a while, then she started talking about you. How arrogant you were. You were so sure you were brighter, smarter, more intellectual than anyone. How you were always correcting her. "He thinks he's so much, and he's nothing," she said. "He doesn't even have a decent family!"

"Yes, he does." I was getting crosser and crosser with Judy. I knew you came from a poor family, that your father drove a beat-up truck and went around picking up stuff from other people's garbage and throwouts. And once I saw you downtown with your mother and she was wearing a long brown skirt and sneakers with her toes sticking out. But I thought Judy was being stupid, and I told her.

"Oh, now you're starting in on me," she said. And she started to cry. "You think he's so perfect, so wonderful. Oh, I know, don't think I don't know."

It's queer how it's all coming back to me now as I'm writing this. I can smell the tar on the road that day, it was so hot, a hot day in May, and I can almost feel all over again the gravel under my bare feet, and then hear Judy saying, "He's impossible, impossible, you can't say anything to him!"

And then the next thing I remember is being in my room, it's night, it's cool, and it's raining outside. And I'm thinking to myself, *Well, even if Judy and Bill don't get together again, I'll still get to see him.*

But I never did. I can't believe it sometimes. You're so real to me, Bill. I can *see* you perfectly clearly in my mind, and yet—are you there, Bill? If I don't actually see you, do you still exist?

121

Dear Bill, Remember Me?

Dear Bill,

Glancing through the newspaper the other day, I noticed the announcement of your marriage to Lucille Lacy Heller Marginy, and I want to congratulate you—

Dear Bill,

A funny thing happened last week. I was out driving with my girlfriend, Randy, and we were on Rock Cut Road and suddenly we passed your house, a little pink house sitting back there behind that old cemetery, with your father's truck parked nearby, ~~and all that old junk in the yard~~ and all of a sudden I remembered that you once took me to your house. I met your brother, Tim, and your sister, Nancy. And we had gingersnaps and milk. But the funny thing is that I hadn't even been on Rock Cut Road in years, and then, the way coincidences happen, yesterday my mother saw the announcement of your marriage in the newspaper. "Mr. and Mrs. Clarence Heller of Woodchuck Hill Road, DeWitt, announce the marriage of their daughter, Lucille Lacy Heller Marginy to William Youngman, Jr., of Rock Cut Road, Jamesville."

My mother said, "Do you remember Judy's old boyfriend, Kathy? Bill Youngman?"

So I said, "Sure." And I laughed because she could even ask me such a question. Then she passed the newspaper over to me.

And she said, "Well, it's quite a jump from Rock Cut Road to Woodchuck Hill Road. I don't think there's a house out there on Woodchuck Hill Road under fifty thousand."

Oh, why am I saying all this to you? It sounds so snobby and stupid! Bill, I just can't get this letter to you right. I want to say so many things, and it's all coming out wrong. It sounds like I care one way or the other where you were born, and I don't. I don't! I—

Dear Bill,

Why did you do it? I keep wondering, why? Are you in love with her? But she's so old. And you said to me, You better let me know when you're sixteen, I want to be there. You said it, and I believed you, Bill! I'm growing up, I'm nearly sixteen, I'm nearly there, if only you'd waited another year!

Bill, why didn't you write me even once? Just a postcard would have been okay. Or a call to say, Hello, how are you, Bitsy, what are you doing, what are you thinking . . .

If I told you all the times I made up conversations you and I could have—if you knew all the letters I've wanted to write you. What if I had written them? Would you have done it? Married her? Oh, God, I know I'm being an absolute jerk, but, Bill—

Dear Bill,

I love you and have ever since I knew you. I don't think I'll ever forget you or stop lov—

123

Dear Bill, Remember Me?

Dear Bill,

The other day I noticed an announcement of your marriage in the newspaper. We were friends a long time ago, and so I want to wish you the best of everything. Peace.

Kathy (Bitsy) Kalman

Chocolate Pudding

Chocolate pudding is my favorite dessert. When it's on the menu in the school cafeteria, I order four or five puddings in those little brown cups, and eat nothing else for lunch. At home, I cook my own chocolate pudding, and when it's cooled enough for that lovely silky skin to come over the top—chocolate skin, I call it—I often eat it straight from the pot. I eat the soft puddingish part first, saving the chocolate skin for last.

I always offer Dad and Uncle some pudding, but neither one is ever interested. They don't eat much, anyway. When they're drinking, I don't believe they eat at all; betweentimes, they'll eat a hunk of cheese, some bread, a few boiled potatoes, sometimes a piece of fruit. Although they're brothers, they haven't the same interests (except for the drinking), nor the same sort of disposition, nor do they look alike. Uncle hasn't Dad's wild mop of red hair, or Dad's white, freckled skin, or Dad's blue eyes, either. (I often think of Dad years ago, when he met my mother and they loved each other—his eyes really blue then, not glaring and watery, and his red hair, and that beautiful jaunty smile. Uncle says girls always liked Dad.) Uncle is shorter and stouter than Dad, brown hair, brown eyes, even his skin is a sort of neutral, light-tannish color. Uncle looks as he is: calm; I've never seen him lose his temper.

Uncle's mad for oranges the way I am for chocolate pudding. When I was a little girl, whenever Uncle took out the curved paring knife from the silverware pitcher and sat down at the table with an orange, I'd come in as close as I could, leaning on his leg to watch, fascinated, as he slowly took off the peel in a perfect spiral.

"Let me have it, please, Uncle," I'd plead, hopping up and down.

"You want a bite of my orange, Chrissy?" he'd say, dividing the orange perfectly in half with the flat of his thumb poked through the center.

"No, Uncle, no! No orange. The peel! Please, Uncle."

"The peel?" he'd say, as if sincerely astonished at such a bizarre request.

When Uncle gave me the peel, and he always did after only a moment of teasing, I'd go under the table with it, near Uncle's feet, and play Eskimo House. There was snow all around, but the Eskimo people inside their orange igloo were cozy and eating spaghetti out of a can the way Uncle, Dad, and I did in winter when the snow plastered itself in little bunches and clumps against the windows, and the wind shrieked across the flat fields outside our wooden trailer.

Our trailer is one long, narrow room. We do our cooking on a two-burner hotplate, we have a refrigerator, table, three chairs, an electric heater, a sink. No more, no less than we need, as Uncle says. Our privy is out back, fifteen feet from the well, as required by state law. Uncle and Dad sleep on the pullout couch, while I used to have a cot with chairs shoved against it to keep me from falling out. But now Uncle and Dad have built a wall across the back of the trailer, making a room for me. They built in a bed, desk, a few shelves. There's a window over my bed. Sometimes when Uncle and Dad are away, I sit on my bed eating chocolate pudding from the pot and looking out the window into the fields.

One afternoon some years ago (I must have been about ten), I came off the school bus, my stomach hollow with hunger, and rushed down our dirt road. My coat was half on, my shoes were untied. I banged on the trailer as I ran alongside it. "Dad? Uncle? Are you there?" The trailer was empty; I went to the cupboard where we kept the chocolate pudding, always Migh-T-Fine in the little white cardboard box with red letters. There was no chocolate pudding. Disbelievingly, I pulled out everything, flinging around boxes and tins. Rage bubbled up in me, thickened, spilled over.

"Damn it, Dad, you did the shopping last week," I shouted. "Damn you. Damn you, damn you, you forgot my chocolate pudding!" I threw myself down on my bed

127

and as I did I thought of the ingredients of chocolate pudding, which were the first words I'd learned to read: *sugar, cornstarch, cocoa* . . . each word carrying a magical, mysterious weight as fine, powdery, and sweet as the granules themselves.

Revived, alert, excited, I got up and dumped cups of cornstarch, cocoa, and sugar together in a pot. I made a terrible mess, bitter and gluey, which I threw out in disgust. Then I started again. And gradually, over the next weeks, I learned to make chocolate pudding properly.

Now I make my own pudding all the time. I vary it, depending on my mood, thin and creamy, or very sweet, or thick, or dark as night. My only regret is that neither Dad nor Uncle shares my pleasure in chocolate pudding. "We've no taste for chocolate," Uncle says. "Though your mother liked it very well."

When my mother was alive, which wasn't even till I was two years old, she and Dad and I lived in an apartment over the drugstore in Middle Square. In my room, tacked up on the wall next to my bed, I have a few snapshots from that time. Often I lie on my stomach across my bed, staring at those pictures, trying to know the people in them. One is of my father sitting on a couch, holding a baby—me—rather stiffly on his knee. He is wearing glasses and his hair falls down over his forehead. He has a serious, almost desperate, look of intensity on his face as he stares straight into the camera that my mother held. Then there is another picture of him and my mother, standing in front of their new car.

Chocolate Pudding

My mother is shading her eyes from the sun, bending a little, smiling and squinting. She is wearing a long, full skirt, shoes with pointed toes, a blouse with buttons down the front. Her hair is flying out to one side, as is her skirt. My father is grinning, he's got his arm around her, he looks jaunty, arrogant, a stranger to me, as strange as my mother.

It was after my mother died that Dad and I moved in with Uncle in the trailer. The two of them cared for me and brought me up. "You look just like your mother," Uncle told me so many times. "Very much like. Except for the hair," he always added. My hair is quite long, reddish; in this way I take after Dad.

How calm Uncle is. I've never heard him raise his voice. One hot summer night when the cicadas were screaming a car drove fast up our road, billowing dust behind it, and a bag of rotting garbage flew straight at the trailer.

"The world is a very ignorant place," was all Uncle said as we cleaned up the slimy mess. "That's a fact, Chrissy." Another time some boys shot out our windows with BB guns, and Uncle called in the State Troopers. Two of them came, very big men in gray uniforms with broad hats and guns holstered at their waists. They walked around the trailer, looking at the windows. They seemed to know Uncle and called him Jack in serious voices, behind which I heard something else that I couldn't identify, but which made me pace angrily behind them.

"Jack," they said, "sure you didn't do this yourself one night, Jack? When you were soaked? You sure, Jack?"

Even then, Uncle didn't get angry.

But I did. I went all cold and shaking. "I was here, right here, in the trailer," I said, "when they drove past and shot at us. Are you going to accuse me of doing it? Are you? *Are you?*"

"Chrissy," Uncle said, putting his hand on my shoulders. "Chrissy, now, Chrissy." His voice, even, calm, soothing, went around my rage, enclosed it, kept it from bursting beyond control. I believe Uncle has the same effect on Dad.

Even if someone cheats them out of their rightful pay, Uncle won't get angry. He says it's not worth it. He and Dad hire out to work as a team, doing odd jobs for the people hereabouts. They'll clean out cellars, tear down old buildings, mix cement, repair roofs, or do the milking for a farmer called away from the farm. They never leave any job before it's finished, and they give good work for their pay. At the end of a working day, they come home, take out the bills and coins they've earned and put them into the tomato juice can we keep on the top shelf of the cupboard.

In January the weather was bitter. Morning after morning, I woke to see my window opaque with frost flowers. Still, Dad and Uncle went out to work often and the tomato juice can was stuffed to the brim with bills and coins. The last day of January was so cold that as I ran down our frozen rutted lane for the school bus the inside of my nose felt fragile as glass. But that night in our trailer it was cozy, the electric heater humming, as I did my homework and Dad listened to Radio Australia on short wave. Uncle was in a mood to talk. "Your mother loved cold weather like this, Chrissy. There was nothing she liked so much as a walk in the cold or a snowball fight."

"My mother was fun to be with?"

"Oh, yes, Ellen was a lovely girl, cheerful and laughing. Nothing got her down. Isn't that right?" he asked Dad. But Dad was lost in some other thought.

"The day I see you take a drink, Chrissy," Dad said, "is the day I'm through with living."

Tears came to his eyes. He put his head down on the table. (Once Dad was very strong—Uncle has told me so.) I've seen him cry many times, drinking does it to him. When I was younger I'd shake his arm, pleading with him not to cry. Crying myself.

But now I'm sixteen, and something hardened in me. "Quit that crying, Dad, just quit it."

Uncle tossed his orange peel into the garbage bag near the door.

Dad lifted his head. He's half blind in one eye, from what I don't know as he refuses to go to a doctor. He wears very thick glasses behind which his eyes, red-veined, seem to glare, but it's only that he's trying to see.

"Get me the cigarettes, Chrissy." He lit up.

"Let me have a puff," I said.

In school, girls are always collecting in the lav or standing around outside the building to sneak a smoke behind their hands. "Chrissy, got a ciggy?" they'll say, because they know I always carry half a pack or so with me. We bend our heads together, lighting up, then pass the cigarette around. It's very easy and friendly, and once in a while I'll wonder if it might go beyond this to a real friendship. It never has.

"I'm sorry," I said after a bit to Dad. "For yelling."

"Oh, it's a good thing you did. I cry too easily these days. I need someone to yell at me."

"Well, don't expect me to make a habit of it." I mashed out the cigarette in the sink. "Uncle can yell at you."

"Oh, not me," Uncle said hastily, "not me," and then, for some reason, we all three laughed.

Toward the end of February, the cold eased, and as March came in I saw the restlessness coming over Dad and Uncle. Dad listening to his broadcasts for only a few moments, then standing up, scratching his arms and his neck, whispering to himself. And Uncle putting down his book, picking it up, putting it down again. After a while, not picking it up at all.

There were chunks of dirty ice piled at the sides of the road where I waited for the school bus, while the sun, thin as a slice of cucumber, still threw enough warmth to burn into my scalp. I felt the restlessness myself, and longed for something. But what?

One night the wind blew with such force, such screaming and wailing through the trees and around the corners of the trailer, such rattling of the windows and shaking of the boards that I couldn't sleep. I sat up in bed and pressed my face to the cold window, trembling and thrilled. I stayed that way for hours before finally falling asleep.

In the morning I felt stupid with tiredness. The wind had died. The sky was blue and calm. Sheets of light poured from the sky, and the sight of a tree, white against the sun, its branches swollen with buds, agitated me in a strange and painful way. Something will happen today, I thought, as I climbed on the bus. Something will happen. The bus jolted forward. The smell of wet mittens and peanuts came to me. Diane Lucas sat down next to me and told me about the wind blowing the roof off her cousin Eddy's barn last night. "They came banging on our door at three o'clock in the morning," she said happily. I nodded, looking at her little pointed chin and delicate white teeth.

In school, the morning passed slowly. The classrooms were all too hot. I leaned my head on my hand. I couldn't remember why I had been so agitated, so feverish with excitement. I drew rows of little cups across a piece of paper and wrote CHOCOLATE PUDDING, shading the letters carefully.

In the cafeteria at lunch time the menu featured sloppy joes and chocolate pudding. I ordered four chocolate puddings and took the cups on a tray to a table in the corner of the lunchroom. I said hello to the others at the table and skinned the top off my first pudding. Slowly I ate the soft insides, cleaning out the little brown dish thoroughly. The kids were talking about Mrs. Fannon, the Latin teacher. "God, she's fierce," Melissa Maguire said. "You have her, don't you, Chrissy?"

"Doesn't everyone?" I said. They laughed. It was a saying in Peter V. Newsome High that you hadn't been educated till Margaret Fannon had called you a nincompoop, a mental incompetent, and utterly beyond redemption.

Saving the chocolate skins in my empty dish, I continued working on the puddings. I had gone through a phase a few years before when I had knocked myself out smiling at Melissa and Debby Pearce, joining their conversations and finding clever things to say about teachers and other kids. I walked in the halls with them, and played on their teams in gym. Once or twice Melissa—or was it Debby?—said something about calling me up. But of course we had no phone. After a while, without anything being said, without anything having happened, one way or the other, I again went my own way.

"I hear Fannon never gives anything over a B," Debby said. "I don't see why anyone takes her classes. A *B!* That would ruin my average."

"Oh, you only have to know how to get around her," Neil Rosencranz said, winking at me. "It's a challenge."

I went on eating my chocolate pudding. Far back in my mind, behind the chatter, the scrape of dishes, the crinkling of sandwich wrappers, I heard the fierce moaning of the wind as it gnawed at the trailer, and I thought of Dad and Uncle sleeping on the pullout couch, their boots tumbled together, safe in the trailer, enclosed, protected. But at the same moment, perhaps for the first time, I thought how frail the trailer was, how weather-beaten the boards, how flimsy the putty that held the windows in place, and I imagined the trailer crumpling in on itself like a deflated paper bag.

Carefully I took the chocolate skin off the last pudding and added it to the others. Two more boys sat down at the table. One of them, Teddy Finkel, had six chocolate puddings on his tray. "Look at that," Debby Pearce said. "Everyone! Look at Teddy Finkel's tray!" Everyone did. "Now look at Chrissy's tray. Isn't that unbelievable?"

"Weird," Melissa said. "It's a convention of chocolate pudding freaks."

Teddy Finkel looked over at me with interest. He had a long bony face and dark hair parted in the middle. "Are you that way about chocolate pudding, too?" We had gone to the same schools for years, but rarely spoken to each other.

"Yes, I like chocolate pudding," I said. I still hadn't eaten the chocolate skins.

"We chocolate pudding freaks don't *like* chocolate pudding, we *revere* it," Teddy Finkel said, digging into a pudding with gusto. In two seconds he'd cleaned it up and started on another. I kept my head down. When I glanced up, his eyes were on me. His expression was mild, playful, curious. He seemed to be asking me a question, or was that my imagination? I felt stifled, breathless. I wanted to throw off my sweater and push away the tray. I ate the last of the chocolate skins and left the cafeteria.

Later that afternoon I saw Teddy Finkel coming toward me in the hall near the science room. He raised his hand and, as he passed, said, "The secret word is chocolate pudding."

I thought of him as the bus jogged me homeward. Again that curious, stifling heat rose behind my ribs. When I got off the bus I cut across the fields toward the trailer. The sun had warmed our road and turned it to muck. The fields were soggy on top, still frozen beneath.

In the trailer I kicked off my drenched shoes and sang one of the old World War II songs Dad and Uncle liked. "When the lights go on again all over the world, when the boys come home again all over the world . . ." I looked out the window for Dad and Uncle, wondering if they were working today.

It grew dark and still they hadn't come home. I had a pot of coffee ready for them on the stove. I did my homework. The clock ticked louder than necessary. Finally I thought of checking the tomato juice can. It was empty, except for a five-dollar bill. So they were gone. Drinking. For a moment my face felt encased in ice, like a spring puddle covered with a skin of ice that wrinkles and crackles at the touch of a foot. The touch of Uncle's voice calling "Chrissy," the sound of Dad's terrible cough outside in the wet darkness, and my ice, too, would crack.

There now, Chrissy, the world is a foolish place. Don't try to figure it out.

Yes, Uncle.

I thought of the wind last night, the frozen fields, that pale burning sun, the tense anticipation that had gripped me like a fever. How sure I'd been that something was going to happen! Yes, and this was it. I poured a cup of coffee and drank it down.

The next day, as I was leaving school and heading for the bus, Teddy Finkel caught me by the arm and said in my ear, "Chocolate pudding." I looked at him, unsmiling. I felt wintry, frozen.

On the school bus I heard the laughter and jokes of the other kids as if from a distance. I thought of nothing, as if I were half asleep. Perhaps I was. I had slept poorly the night before, jerking awake many times, listening, listening, listening to the darkness and the night. When I got off the bus I walked slowly down the muddy road, my booksack slung over one shoulder. Suddenly I started running, and I banged on the side of the trailer the way I used to do, calling "Dad? Uncle?" I knew, however, that the trailer would be empty.

Several days passed. Each afternoon when I returned from school I felt first sick with disappointment, then fiercely glad they hadn't come back. They would be weepy with remorse, ill, weak, bruised, smelling of vomit. All the money would be gone. I would have to make them food, heat water for them to wash, and take their stinking clothes to the laundromat. Dad would cry day and night, tears would leak from his very pores. *Forgive me Chrissy forgive your old father he's no good no good do you forgive me Chrissy Chrissy I've hurt you . . .*

Oh, I knew it all. I knew just how it would be. How they would smell. How they would look. How the sight of them would make it difficult for me to breathe.

"Stay away," I raged aloud one night, pacing up and

down the trailer, reaching out to bang my fists against the walls. "Stay away, both of you! Do you think I want you back, smelling of vomit? Stay away, I tell you," I screamed. "Do you hear me, you two?"

I slept well that night. I woke up once and listened to the quiet of the trailer, the quiet outside. Quite near, an owl hooted, the one that sounds like a horse whinnying. I breathed easily, in and out, in and out, and stretched my legs till my toes touched the bottom of the bed. My head was muzzy with dreams and I fell asleep again, at once.

In the morning, rain drummed lightly on the tin roof of the trailer and smeared the windows. Crows cawed far away.

When I arrived at school, Teddy Finkel was at the water fountain on the first floor. Straightening, he saw me and said, "Chocolate!" Later, we passed each other again in the hall near the gym. Almost simultaneously, we both said, "Pudding."

He reversed himself to walk with me. "I guess we've worn that joke out," he said.

"Why do we keep bumping into each other?" I said. He followed me into the library and sat down where I did, at one of the long tables under a window. I took out my biology notebook.

"You going to work?" he said.

"That was the general idea."

"A better idea is to talk to me. Tell me what you like besides chocolate pudding."

"Oh—" I shrugged. I didn't know what to say. Did

he mean what other foods I liked, or what else I liked to do besides eat chocolate pudding? I flipped open my notebook.

"Nice neat work," he said, leaning over to look. "You like bio?"

"Yes." I started drawing an amoeba in pencil, just lightly, till I felt I had it right.

He pulled a book off a shelf behind him, opened it, and stared straight into it. "You're not really very friendly, are you?" he said.

"Because I don't flirt?"

"I don't think smiling is exactly flirting," he said. "I mean, we had a little joke going, a little thing between us, the chocolate pudding, and you never once smiled."

I bent my head over my notebook. I felt something fasten itself, like a bone, or a hook, in my throat. I made another little squiggly line on my amoeba.

"Listen, you know what my whole name is?" he said. "Theodore Roosevelt Finkel. My mother named me after him. She really did. Listen, I don't tell that to everyone. It's an offering, a friendship offering."

I turned my head a fraction and looked into his eyes. They were the color of prunes, that shiny soft black of stewed prunes, an amazing color.

"What are you thinking about now?" he said.

"I'm thinking that I promised myself to get this bio notebook caught up, and with you bothering me I never will. And I'm thinking that your eyes are really strange, and how long is it going to take for you to get sick of sitting around getting nowhere with me?"

"But I don't want to get somewhere with you," he said. "I just want to get to know you."

"Why?"

"Why?" he repeated.

"Yes. Why?" I really wanted to know.

"You're not like other girls, are you? I mean, you really aren't like other girls at all, are you?"

I felt suddenly depressed. It was true. I'd known it for a long time. I wasn't like other girls, like Melissa or Debby, who knew how to talk to boys easily, how to laugh and say amusing things. "I'm sorry." I flipped senselessly through my bio book.

"Sorry! Don't say that. Don't be *sorry*, Chrissy." He put his hand into my biology book, flattening it out. "You're not a phony, that's all I meant. God, some of the hypocritical types around here—they make me want to puke." Two red spots of excitement appeared high on his cheekbones. Then the bell rang, and I started pushing my papers together. I hadn't done a bit of work, but it didn't matter, the trailer would be quiet again tonight without Dad and Uncle.

"Well, are we friends?" Teddy said, walking out of the library with me.

"I don't know." I hurried up the stairs.

"You mean that, don't you?"

"Yes," I said impatiently. "Why would I say it, otherwise?"

"God, I like you," he said. "I really like you! We're going to be friends. Definitely." He grabbed my arm. "What are you doing after school?"

"Going home."

"I'll come with you."

"I go on the bus, school bus."

"I know."

"I live fifteen miles out."

"Okay."

I stopped in front of Mrs. Fannon's classroom. "How will you get back?"

He raised his thumb and jerked it across his shoulder. A shiver crossed my neck. I shifted my books from one arm to the other. At last I said, "I don't know if I want you to come home with me. I don't know, I just don't know!"

"Listen," he said. "Listen—" He touched my shoulder. "It's all right. Really." He peered into my face seriously and reassuringly. Then he walked down the corridor.

After school he was waiting outside where the buses were lined up at the curb. "Hi," he said. It was still raining. I felt the other kids looking at us. I climbed on the bus.

"He's with me," I said to the driver, tilting my head back at Teddy. We took two seats toward the rear of the bus.

"Hi, Chrissy!" Diane Lucas called in an excited voice, as she stared at Teddy. "Got company?"

"It must be a drag taking the bus every day," Teddy said. He leaned back in the seat, folding his arms across his chest.

"I don't mind. I'm used to it."

The bus filled up. Kids were yelling to each other. Someone blew up a lunch bag and popped it. "All right, you kids, settle down," Mrs. Johnson, the bus driver, yelled. Nobody paid any attention.

The bus left the school grounds, drove through Middle Square, past the bank with its fluted columns, the supermarket, a dress shop, the laundromat. A few people hurried through the rain, shoulders hunched. I stared at everything through the rain-smeared windows as if seeing it all for the first time, conscious of Teddy looking across my shoulder. On the outskirts of Middle Square, we drove by a set of stone gates with a white arch over them lettered STONY ACRES. Behind the arch I caught a glimpse of big houses, wet clean road, and clipped lawns, soggy and glistening.

"That's where I live," Teddy said. "Did you ever hear such a phony name? Stony Acres. Ha!" The bus swept past. "Are you at the end of the line?"

"Not quite. A few kids live farther out than me."

"Do you usually do homework or something on the ride?"

"Usually."

"Well, don't let me stop you. Just do what you usually do, you know?"

I shook my head. I was looking at his eyes again, that strange dark soft color. "It's okay. I don't have that much."

He started telling me about the piano lessons his folks had given him years ago. "It was like I was playing

142

with my feet, I drove my piano teacher crazy. My parents wanted me to have a certain basic musical education. I kept at it for five years. Five years! My parents don't give up easily. Five years of torture for my piano teacher."

I laughed. I forgot to look out the window. I forgot how disastrous this afternoon would turn if Uncle and Dad were home, needing me to help them sober up. It was only when Teddy followed me off the bus and walked beside me down our road that I remembered. I dodged puddles and approached the trailer slowly. The pickup truck was parked, as always, to one side. That meant nothing. They never took the pickup when they went off.

"What are those TV's doing outside?" Teddy said, pointing to the two TV sets stacked one atop the other at one end of the trailer. Uncle had thrown a short piece of canvas over the top of them and forgotten them.

"Some people gave them to Uncle and Dad in part payment for work they did. We have no place for them inside." I opened the door and stood there, listening. The trailer was silent. Everything as I had left it in the morning.

"Can I come in out of the rain?" Teddy said from behind me, and I moved out of the doorway.

"Come in—please." I put my books down on the table. I saw how shabby everything was. How bare and worn.

"Is this it?" Teddy prowled the length of the trailer in four strides. He reached up and touched the ceiling, then stretched out his arms, almost touching the walls. "This is it?"

"Yes."

"You do everything right here—cook, eat, sleep, your homework, everything?"

"Yes." I folded my arms across my chest.

"God!" His eyes were shining. "It's wonderful. It's so honest. So essential." He indicated the door to my room. "What's that? A bathroom?"

"My room."

"Can I see?"

"All right." As soon as I said it, I felt very scared in a way I couldn't understand.

Teddy put his head inside the door, then stepped in. For a moment there was silence. I felt chilled.

"Chrissy," he said. "This is great. This is fantastic. You know what, this is exactly like a room I've dreamed of having."

"Don't—" I said.

"My God, for years I've had this dream of a perfect room, just plain, a bed or cot, maybe even just a mattress on the floor, a plain desk, some shelves, a couple drawers." His hand sliced the air, as if cutting his dream room off before it got too big.

I sat down on my bed, staring around at everything, as if seeing it for the first time. The same thing that happened on the bus. Teddy sat down next to me. "I've always liked my room," I said.

Our faces were very close. He had a faint mustache

144

growing across his upper lip and he smelled soapy. "Would it be all right—you wouldn't be mad if I kissed you?"

Our lips touched. I had never known such sweetness. I leaped up, frightened, filled with a crazy happiness. It seemed I might once have felt this way, but when? When? I laughed out loud and pulled Teddy up. "Let's have some chocolate pudding!"

I got out the cocoa tin, the sack of sugar, the box of cornstarch, and measured the ingredients into a pan. I poured in milk and stirred the mixture over the hotplate. Teddy hovered at my shoulder, watching. As the pudding thickened and came to a boil, I reached into the cupboard over the hotplate for two dessert cups. "Sometimes I eat it straight out of the pot," I said.

"Why not now?"

"You're company."

He put his hand to his chest, pretended to stagger back, knocking against the broom closet. "Ooow! You know how to hurt a man. Company!"

I took the pot off the stove and set it down in the middle of the table. I took two spoons from the pitcher and we sat down across from each other. The chocolate pudding was thick and shiny. Teddy dipped in his spoon and took a taste. He closed his eyes and hummed. "I've never had chocolate pudding like this."

"We should have taken off the chocolate skin," I said, a bit regretfully.

He dipped up spoonful after spoonful. "You're a genius,

145

a chocolate pudding genius. Chrissy, I swear it, after this, never again chocolate pudding in a tin."

"A tin?" I said. I felt extraordinarily happy.

"My mother the tennis player buys chocolate pudding in little tins," Teddy said. "You know. They're in the market. Little tins about so big. Puddin'-In-A-Tin, it's called. Evil people somewhere have plotted this conspiracy against chocolate pudding lovers of the world. They squeeze something thick, gluey, and brown into little tins and label it chocolate pudding. And to think that, till this moment, I had no idea of the extent of their evil conspiracy! True, I knew tinned chocolate pudding tasted different than school-cafeteria chocolate pudding, but their diabolical cleverness succeeded in making me believe it *was* chocolate pudding, even if of an inferior grade. But this—" He shook his head and dipped again into the pot.

"Now that I have tasted true chocolate pudding, I've seen the light. Praise the Lord, I've seen the light! And it's clear now that what has been packed into chocolate pudding tins and passed off on the world as chocolate pudding is really—" He paused, looked at me seriously, said, "Are you ready for this shocking revelation?"

"Ready," I said.

"Then listen closely. That stuff in those tins is really hippopotamus mud."

"Hippopotamus mud?"

"Absolutely. Mud in which hippos have been rolling and playing for days to get it to the proper consistency.

146

I see it all now!" He picked up the pot and scraped the inside.

I tipped back on my chair, watching Teddy. He was wearing a soft, clean, denim shirt, and worn-looking jeans. His jacket, which he had tossed over the other chair, was fur-lined. An image of his house suddenly sprang into my mind. It would have eight or ten rooms, each one larger than our whole trailer, a fireplace, wall oven, a garage for two cars, and two cars in the garage. It would have a patio in back, and big double glass doors that slid open. His mother played tennis and his father was, perhaps, a doctor.

"Is your father a doctor, and do you have a fireplace in your house?"

"No and qualified yes. He's a lawyer and there are two fireplaces. One in the parents' bedroom, one in the living room."

"Two," I said.

"Yes. And more rooms than we need. And furniture, and all kinds of garbage. Conspicuous, wasteful, disgusting consumption. Let's not talk about my house or my family."

"Don't you like them?"

"Actually, I do. But the way we live—" He drew his thin shoulders together. "You people have the right idea. Everything basic. Where's the john?" He stood up.

"Privy outside. Go right around the side of the trailer. You can't miss it."

"My God!" His face glowed as he rushed outside. I

let my chair down onto the floor, took the pot to the sink and filled it with water to soak. Teddy came back in, shutting the trailer door carefully behind him, shaking rain off his shoulders and his head. "Do you use that in winter, too?"

"Yes," I said, "but at night I use a pot if I have to."

"It's what we all have to come back to." He leaned against the table. "We Americans use too much of everything. Too much gas, too much electricity, too much food, too much of all the natural resources. The figures per capita compared to the rest of the world are really gross. Wait a second, I'll show you an article—" He dug into his pockets, taking out a handful of change, a few bills, keys, scraps of paper, throwing it all down on the table, talking about the world food crisis and how it could be solved. "Well, I can't find it, but you know what I mean." He pushed his hair back behind his ears. "You're doing things right. Basic. Down to the bone. It's terrific."

We went on talking. I made him laugh by telling him how I learned to read from chocolate pudding boxes when I was about four years old. It got dark outside. We drank milk, and ate bread with peanut butter. I turned on a light. It was warm in the trailer. That strange feeling of happiness crept over me again. It was an amnesiac feeling, as if happiness had made me forget all sorts of important things. After a few moments it came to me that I had forgotten to think about Uncle and

Dad. I sat straighter, alert, listening for them in the rainy darkness outside.

Teddy stood up. "I really have to go." I gave him directions for getting out to the highway. He didn't think he'd have any trouble getting a ride back to the Square. "If I get stuck, I can always call my mother from a gas station and she'll come pick me up. She's a good kid, my mother." He took my hand. "Anyway. Right?"

"Basic," I said.

"Chocolate pudding," he said.

"Okay. Chocolate pudding."

"Remember that. The two most important words in the world. Choc-o-late pud-ding." In the midst of our silliness, we kissed again.

Teddy left. I sat down at the table and opened my notebook. I found myself listening, as I had every night lately, for sounds which might be Uncle and Dad returning. I was chilly and got a sweater. How lonely the rain sounded tapping on our tin roof. Suddenly, I ran to the door and pulled it open.

"Theodore Roosevelt Finkel," I called. He was gone. I ran into the road. It was dark. Rain fell heavily all around. "Teddy," I called. "Teddy!"

"Over here!" His voice came from a distance. "Chrissy —you okay?"

"Okay," I replied. "See you tomorrow." The rain seemed to wash away my voice. I put my hands around my mouth, and called as loud as I could, "Chocolate pudding!" And from a distance, Teddy's voice came singing out of the darkness, *"Choc-o-late pud-ding."*

Guess Whose Friendly Hands

Louise had had the cat dream again. She woke up with the echo of her dream voice shouting in her head . . . *dyed GREEN?* Her amputated leg was aching. Sometimes the leg that wasn't there hurt more than anything else. Sometimes the pain centered in her belly, more terrible than anything she could ever have imagined. Drugs—she loved drugs now. She, who had never taken an aspirin.

She was eighteen, and dying. She was quite sure she was dying, although nobody had said this in so many words. Not her mother, Mary Amelia Pesco, nor her sister, Beth, nor Martha Finley, the only one of her friends who still came occasionally to sit by her bed, to tell her lies, and talk about the things they'd do when Louise was up and around again. "Did you hear about the mob at Green Lakes on July Fourth? Did you see the picture in the *Herald Journal*? Next year, Lou, we'll go together, you, me, the whole gang. What a riot. Danny got drunk on two bottles of beer, the jackass." And later, as she was leaving, "You're looking terrific, I mean . . . really better than before . . . I mean, you are . . ."

The word death was never mentioned. Louise was "sick." She was "improving," or "getting better," or "recovering." That's what they said.

She had been dying for two years. Perhaps longer. But certainly for two years. On a January day, one of those metallic winter days when the air is hard and glinting, Louise had stepped off a Salina Street bus, stepped over a mound of dirty snow, and fallen. Gone down like a felled tree. She had been unable to get up.

"Come on, Lou, quit kidding," Martha said. They had been downtown, it was Saturday, and they'd amused themselves touring the stores, Dey's, Sibley's, Flah's, snorting derisively over the prices of clothing neither of them could afford.

"I'm not kidding, I can't get up." Louise had laughed disbelievingly. "My legs feel drunk."

"Maybe you sprained something." Martha put her mittened hands around Louise's ski jacket and hauled at her. No use. Louise was dead weight there on the frozen sidewalk. Hank Martelli, the barber, had come out of his little shop and helped Martha. They had half dragged, half carried Louise the three blocks home. "I feel like such a dope," she kept saying.

Two years of doctors, operations, therapy. Money and hope inextricably mingled. The one in increasingly short supply, the other manufactured afresh every morning.

Louise often thought of them, money and hope: money was green; hope, blue. Why blue? Because it was her favorite color? She'd had a blue dress long ago, polka dotted, with a little round white collar. Also a blue glass cat, and a blue lucite comb and brush set.

The comb and brush, enclosed in a stiff plastic case with a red snap, had been a birthday present given her by Beth, bought at Daw's Cut Rate Store for $1.75. Louise should know: she'd lent Beth 75 cents of that money and, in fact, taken her to the store, as she took Beth everywhere. It had been Louise's tenth birthday. The comb had snapped in half one morning as Louise dragged it through her thick, wiry hair—and the brush —? The brush, too, was gone, but Louise couldn't remember what had happened to it. Yet she had always remembered everything! Telephone numbers, birthdays, dental appointments, how much Ma owed to what stores, and when it had better be paid to avoid those letters that said: LAST WARNING. WE ARE FORCED TO HAND THIS ACCOUNT OVER TO A COLLECTION AGENCY. But now—now, she couldn't remember a simple thing like what had happened to the blue hairbrush. No, she took it back! She didn't love drugs. She hated them!

It was a summer morning. The weight of moist heat and decay pressed down on Louise's body. Beneath her neck, her pillow was damp. A pale pink-striped sheet, sweet as candy cane, covered her. She twitched at the sheet. What had happened to that brush? Her face went rigid with the effort to remember, but her memory balked like a big stubborn dog that sets its behind down on the ground, determined not to move. And there she was, tugging at the leash, but without the strength anymore to make that dog respond to her will—that dog which had once frisked, snapped, jumped, and rolled over at a snap of her fingers. She knuckled her forehead angrily. But even her anger, which used to course through her like a healthy river, was diluted, fuzzed, blurred by drugs and pain.

She pushed herself slowly up in bed till she was leaning against the headboard. Only eight o'clock, and already Syracuse sweltered under sullen skies. For days, thunder had rumbled distantly, like cannon in a far-off war. "Oh, the war, the war," she sighed, not knowing why she said it, and then thinking of all the books she hadn't read yet, books about history, and wars, and the people who had lived through them. But the truth was she hated war books, and war movies, and war news, and military parades and drum rolls. All that military garbage!

She was a pacifist at heart, if not in fact; believed fervently in peaceful ways between human beings, but had always been ready to tear to shreds anyone who might hurt, molest, scare, snare, ambush, trip, or trap her sister. Except herself, of course.

Oh, the fights they had had. She remembered pounding Beth unmercifully, sitting on her head, pushing her down on the floor and trying to walk on her belly. Poor Beth, the baby, the younger sister, the one who had to obey Louise—or else! But now Louise was the helpless one, cared for, babied, everything done for her by Beth and Ma that once she had done so well for herself. She raised her hands into the air. They hung before her eyes, gross, rubbery, inflated. Useless.

"Go away," she said to the hands, shoving them beneath the pink sheet.

There was a knock at the door.

"Good morning," Beth sang, coming in with Louise's breakfast tray in her outstretched hands. Did Louise only imagine that since her illness Beth's walk had changed? Or had it actually become brisker, stronger, each foot set down with new assurance? Beth at sixteen. How buoyant she was. How pretty. How splendid. How perfect. How full of . . . life! She wore a pair of ragged-edged shorts and a green tee shirt with who me? printed across the chest. Her breasts bounced gaily, her protruding blue eyes were calm. She was as Louise had once been; as, sometimes, for fleeting, dreamlike moments, Louise still thought of herself. She hadn't seen herself in a mirror in, oh, five months. Ma had taken the mirror from her room first, then emptied the apartment of mirrors. Big mirrors and small, pocket mirrors, bureau mirrors, even the mirrored door of the bathroom medicine cabinet—all had disappeared.

"I was thinking about that blue comb and brush set you bought me for my tenth birthday," she said.

Beth laughed. "You remember the funniest things."

"I remember throwing that brush at you once when

we had a fight," Louise said. A small shock of triumph made her lie back, close her eyes, and smile. There it was, the memory she wanted. *You big bully*, Beth had screamed in a rage, *you're always telling me what to do, I hate you, you big bully asshole.*

And Louise: *Don't you talk to me like that. I'm in charge here.* Then the brush flying out of her hand, whizzing through the air, straight toward Beth. Smashing against the wall, breaking into pieces. And Beth, sniveling, crying furiously, *I gave you that for your birthday.*

Louise opened her eyes. "Don't you remember that brush, and the fight we had, Beth?"

Beth put the tray down on the table next to Louise's bed. "You know me, I don't remember stuff like that. You're the memory machine in the family. Don't know what Ma and I would do without you."

"You'll learn," Louise said, sipping orange juice.

Beth snapped up the window shade. Had she heard Louise?

"Ugh, another hot day," she said. "Wish it would rain, or something."

Or something.

Louise heard in those words a wistful, painful plea. With all the love in the world, they wished her to die and get it over with. This business of being sick, of slowly dying had gone on too long! It was rude, disgusting, and expensive. No wonder they wouldn't talk about it. No, they wouldn't talk. They didn't say one word. Not one. Not even mumble it under their breath, or whisper it suddenly in the dark on a night when she couldn't sleep because of pain.

And yet, look at her. Look at her. *Look at her!* Her breasts had been taken from her, cut off, one at a time. A leg was gone. Other parts, too. Her flesh had been cut, severed, skewered, implanted, eviscerated. Her face had ballooned into a shapeless swollen moon, and her hair had fallen out in clumps.

Once she had loved her body. It did so well for her. She was nimble, coordinated, a runner, a jumper, a leaper. Her arms and legs were rounded, her shoulders smooth, her belly ticklish as hell. There were only her mother, her sister, herself: three females. They walked around the apartment with or without clothing, dressed, undressed, half dressed, calling to one another. She, the older sister, the responsible one, Ma's right hand, kept Beth in line. When she heard Beth refer to her "peepee," a word she had picked up at school, Louise was shocked in a slightly superior way. "Didn't Ma tell you the right words?" she had demanded. "Didn't I tell you one thousand times? It's ignorant to call yourself by dumb names."

"I heard the boys say pussy," Beth ventured. She was a frail child, without Louise's sturdy, well-coordinated body.

"Forget that," Louise said, but without rancor. She had never been able to feel that such a word was bad. She was crazy about pussycats. Too bad they couldn't have one, but Beth was allergic to everything, sneezing her head off whenever she was around dogs, or cats, or even a little harmless white mouse. No, they had no pets. They had no father. They had no money. They had only one another, mother and daughters. The two girls grew up very close.

"Made your eggs the way you like them, with chives," Beth said.

Louise took a little bite. She had no appetite. Food nauseated her. She didn't even like to look at the eggs, but Beth had made them specially. "You're good, Beth," she said.

"Ah, you'll do the same for me some day. I'll get myself an interesting disease and lie in bed like a queen being waited on by you. Remember how you used to make me tea with milk whenever I got a cold? And let me eat all the chocolate marshmallow cookies I wanted?"

"I remember," Louise said. Every winter Beth had had sniffles, colds, sore throats, a runny nose. Louise, nothing. She would stay home from school to look after Beth, glad for the chance to read, or watch TV, or play checkers with Beth. "You're healthy as a horse," Ma said. And Louise complained, jokingly, that Beth had it all, that she never got a chance to be sick. Now, in two years, Beth hadn't had so much as a sneeze.

Later, Beth came back, took away the breakfast tray, mostly untouched. "Ready for the bedpan?"

"Okay." Louise looked out the window, in order to pretend it was happening to someone else's body. Every day it shamed her that her mother and sister had to carry her body's wastes out of the room. She looked at her reflection in the window. Nightmare face, moonface, stretched tight and shiny. Ma had never realized she had a "mirror" next to her bed. Stiff yellow bristles of new hair. Jack-o'-lantern face. Once she had been pretty. Now her cheeks were tremendous, evilly cheerful.

They lived on the top floor of a two-family, flat-roofed house on Carbon Street. Louise's window looked out on the gray clapboard walls of the house next door. Above the neighbor's roof she could see a small patch of sky, gray today as it had been for a week.

"Maybe it'll rain today," Beth said, again. "This humidity—" She licked around her mouth, licking off the sweat. "Up you go." She took the bedpan, left the room. The toilet flushed down the hall.

She came back, carrying a bowl of warm water. "Hey, I forgot to tell you. Guess who phoned last night?"

"Who?"

"Come on, guess, lazybones." All day Beth played little games with Louise. Guess what we're having for lunch? Guess who I saw downtown? Guess what I found for you in the library? The less Louise ate, the less she could concentrate on reading, and the fewer people she saw, the more cheerfully and insistently Beth played guessing games.

"I don't want to guess, hon."

"Come on, guess! Don't be a party-pooper."

Louise had her private name for Beth's game—Never Say Die. Too bad she couldn't share it with Beth; she really would appreciate it. On boring, rainy afternoons waiting for Ma to come home from work, smearing their fingers over the damp dusty windows, she and Beth would play the cliché game like mad, pat phrases and bromides tripping off their tongues (of course), while they (naturally) shook like jelly with laughter. And the grass is greener on the other side of the fence, there's a silver lining behind every cloud, a rolling stone gathers no moss, and people who live in glass houses should pull down their shades. They could keep that up for hours, even after Ma came home, till she ordered them to stop before she went crazy. Beth: *Bats in her belfry.* Louise: *Don't be disrespectful. She has a wise old head on those young shoulders.* And Ma, half laughing: *Girls, I'm warning you for the last time, I mean it . . .*

Beth plucked a fresh towel from a pile on the bureau, threw it onto the foot of Louise's bed, and took a bar of pink scented soap from a white soap dish. "So? Who do you guess? Who called?"

"Kevin Morris." A boy Louise had known in high school, tall, blond, good-looking, aloof.

"Ho, ho, ho, don't you wish. Try again."

Lenny? But she didn't say his name. He was in California. He'd written her a few letters, really funny letters. After her leg was amputated, she wrote and told him she wasn't the girl she once was. He appreciated that, wrote back, but the last letter had been almost a year ago.

"Guess!"

"Barbara Freelock. Margaret. Susan. Oh, stuff it, Beth, tell me who."

"Frank and Myra Weiss," Beth said, dipping the cloth into the basin of warm water.

"The Weisses? Mr. and Mrs. Weiss?" Louise flapped her swollen hands in the air. "Frank and Myra?"

Beth began washing Louise's neck and face and arms. She smiled. "Yes, Frank and Myra. How many Weisses do we know?"

"Why? Why are they coming?" She pushed Beth's ministering hands away. "Who called them? Why are they coming?"

"To see you," Beth said. "Don't you want them to come? Take it easy, if you don't want them to come—"

"It's all right. I was just surprised. After all this time."

"Well, it is sort of a surprise," Beth said, again washing Louise vigorously, passing over the scarred history of Louise's body as easily as she had once skated down the street. "You know Ruth Petty from Ma's job is Myra Weiss's sister. Remember? I guess Ma mentioned that you were sick, and probably Ruth told Myra. So she called and said they'd stop in for a while to see you." Beth's hair swung over her face. Her cheeks shone with health and lies.

Sick. Just stopping in. Dropping in. Casually. Because she was *sick*. After two years, just *stopping* in?

Why didn't they tell her the truth? Oh, if only they'd tell her! What relief, then; the future known, accepted, acknowledged. Your Future Is Safe in the Friendly Hands of Death. Hello, Death. Listen to me, open the door, let me in. She thought of the absence of pain, the end of debt for Ma, freeing Ma and Beth to live again without secret sorrow, without lies. But hope flew up, buzzed its way into her mind, like a mosquito, tiny but full of poison. Couldn't be kept out. "Beth, why are they really coming?"

"I just told you. To see you."

But you promised. You promised never to lie to me.

Once, with a glance, she could have made Beth stammer; with a word, burst into tears. As skinny girls of six and eight with tight stiff pigtails, hands crossed and clasped, they had sworn themselves to truth forever. "No lies, no secrets, the truth, the whole truth, only the truth," Louise had chanted. "Okay, you say it now, Bethie."

"No lies, no secrets, the truth, the whole truth, only the truth." Beth's face had been solemn, moist, red with fervor.

Their father had lied to them, lied to their mother, had a secret life, had many secrets, had left them all to go to Arizona with another woman and her son. "And remember, we hate Daddy," Louise had instructed.

"Yes, we hate Daddy," Beth repeated.

Every day Louise had herded Beth protectively home from school, touching from time to time the thin coldness of the apartment key which hung on a leather thong around her neck. Ma worked as a punch-press operator in the Mica insulator factory and didn't get home until close to six o'clock. In the silent apartment, Louise leading, Beth following, they hung up their dresses, smoothing them carefully so they could wear them one more day, put on jeans, and then set the table and put three washed potatoes in the potato baker on top of the stove.

Chewing on raw carrots and soft white bread, they would rush down the stairs to play on Carbon Street until they spotted the hurrying, smiling, bulky figure that was Ma. She had never lied to them, either. No lies, no secrets, the truth, the whole truth, and nothing but the truth for Ma and her girls. Till now, when the lies and half-truths, the evasions and secrets spun through the apartment like spider's filament, toughly frail, almost invisible, swaying in the slightest breeze. Louise longed to gather it all up, crush the frail webs in her hand, yet the thought of it made her heart beat up sickeningly into her throat.

Frank Weiss.

Louise had worked in his law office the summer she was fifteen, the job connection made through Ruth Petty, Ma's friend from work. Heat. The air conditioner whining, rug casting up static sparks at her legs, venetian blinds on the window overlooking South Salina Street always half closed. Louise at fifteen, buoyant, naive, yearning, waiting. She had run errands, carried coffee in cardboard containers from the diner across the street, dusted desks, answered the telephone when no one was around, taken messages, read here and there in the law books, called Beth three times a day to be sure she was okay.

"Mr. Weiss—" she said.

"Call me Frank," he said. "I never had a daughter." He

hugged her. He was three times her age, dapper, with a jaunty bouncing step, a small wiry brush mustache. She liked and feared his hugs. She felt him watching her. She began hunching her shoulders protectively around her breasts. She was uncomfortable with him, but when she was away from him, he appeared in her mind gentler, finer, wiser, more interesting.

She told her friend Martha, "I have a thing for older men." Martha stared at her, fascinated. Louise was inspired to go on. She gave a sophisticated sigh. "It must be a father fixation. I'm probably looking for a father substitute. I suppose all my life I'll be helplessly drawn to older men."

In fact, she was relieved when the summer was over, she had collected her last paycheck, and could mention Frank Weiss with a small knowing smile, instead of having to see him every day. And then, that winter, turning sixteen, she met Lenny Cormac. He was a friend of Martha's older brother, Billy. Lenny went to Syracuse University, he was a sophomore, wore size 13 sneakers, carried around a copy of *War and Peace* which he said he was reading for the fifth time, talked a blue streak, kissed Louise like mad, and one night said, "Listen, do you want to try? I mean, listen, I've slept with one girl, so I know something, but I won't kid you, I'm no big swordsman. I mean, that is—you understand?"

She had been startled, delighted, strangely tender. She had thought about it. It wasn't love, but it was experience. She had had so little. She was restless, had crazy moods, could go into mad giggling fits with Beth, or else ignore her for a whole day. "Oh, quit bothering me. You're always following me around! What are we, Siamese twins!"

She decided to find out what sex was all about from Lenny. He shared an apartment with three other SU boys on the fourth floor of a decrepit brown building on University Avenue. It was a dingy little place. The bathroom—little hairs stuck in the soap, grime encrusted on the faucets—was revolting. Lenny's room was more like a closet, no windows, a cot covered with a brown blanket, a wooden desk he'd bought at the Salvation Army downtown, and a bookcase perched on top of the desk. Posters of Greece and Italy, full of light and sun, covered the peeling walls. Jeans and shirts hung limply from hooks on the walls.

They took off their clothes and lay down on the cot. "Okay, what now?" Louise said, agreeably. They both started to laugh. They really got hysterical. Every time they seemed about to stop, one of them would say, "Okay, what now," and they'd be off again. They shouldn't have laughed, they couldn't do anything. Nothing happened! She was just as glad. His belly was so white.

Boys were supposed to be upset about things like that, but Lenny didn't seem to care. They got dressed and drank coffee in the kitchen, then went out and ate hot dogs and French fries at the Carroll's on Marshall Street. Every once in a while they'd look at each other and burst out laughing.

About a month later she'd gone down on the icy sidewalk on Salina Street. For two years there'd been doctors, drugs, hospitals, operations. The thought of the money dazed her. When she tried to talk to Ma about it, she was cut off at once. "Shh! Money! What's money?" Ma's voice was always quiet. "I'm surprised at you, Louise."

"But, Ma, I want to know."

"There's nothing to know. For once, leave the money figuring to me. You just rest and get better."

"Get better?" Ma's hands were squeezing each other, squeezing each other bloodless, her bitten-down fingernails were gray as clamshells.

"That's right. Rest, rest, rest. Take care of yourself, that's all you have to worry about. Okay? Okay, Louise?"

"Okay, Ma." How could she argue with Ma? Hadn't she always done what Ma wanted, been Ma's willing partner, helper, good right hand? No lies, no secrets . . . Money had never been a secret before. Now money couldn't be mentioned. Money and death—the forbidden subjects. Neither word was allowed to pass anyone's lips. Only in her dreams did Louise speak freely, shouting into empty rooms, *Tell me the color of that cat's skin. Why is she dyed green?*

"I dreamed about a green cat last night," she said, as Beth went on washing her body with the patient care of a mother.

"Oh, that reminds me, I had the funniest dream. I don't even remember what it was, something about stuffing myself into a cookie jar, I think! But I woke up laughing from it. Do you ever wake up laughing from your dreams?"

"Beth—" Louise grabbed her sister's hand. "Bethie—"

"Yes?" Beth smiled, her eyes suddenly cautious.

"Won't you . . . will you . . ." Say it. *Louise, you're dying*. Three words were all that was necessary, three words to purge her of fear and uncertainty, of hope and envy more poisonous than the cancer. Three words to tear up the lies that lay between them, sticky as spider's webbing.

"You're sweating." Beth pried open Louise's fingers to release her hand. She rubbed her chest, her hand moving round and round over the white letters, WHO ME? "The heat's getting you, isn't it?" Round and round her hand moved, and she drew in several deep sighing breaths. "It's getting me, too, I think." She went to the bureau for the can of white baby powder. She sprinkled baby powder on Louise's arms and leg, and over her back and belly. "Feels good, doesn't it?"

"Yes. Good. Thanks, Beth."

The day passed slowly. She found it difficult, almost impossible to read anymore. Sometimes she felt the pain gathering itself, coming like a wave from afar, growing in intensity, speeding up, hurling itself against her. There were drugs to take. She dozed. She woke with sourness leaking from the corners of her mouth.

Then it was almost time for the Weisses' visit. "Beth," she called. "Bethie." She pushed the knob on the little bell Beth had bought at the drugstore. "Beth." And when Beth appeared, "A kerchief. A kerchief for my head, please."

Beth tied a pretty blue-figured silk scarf over her

head, behind her neck. She washed Louise again, changed her nightgown, and rubbed lemon-scented cologne stick along her arms and behind her ears. "I'll make up your eyes," she said, hurrying out for the little mascara kit. Working with her tongue caught between her lips, Beth dabbed light blue on Louise's eyelids, mascara on her lashes. "There! Gorgeous. Oh, you have gorgeous eyes, not bug eyes like mine."

"Let me see," Louise said. "Bring me a mirror. Do I look like a clown?"

"You look—perfect," Beth said, turning away, her words falling away, reaching Louise as if shouted from a distant shore.

"I want a mirror." Mirrors told the truth. But just then the doorbell rang. A harsh buzzing. "It must be them. Oh, Beth, take this junk off my eyes!"

Beth clicked the plastic kit closed. "I'll do no such thing."

"Beth—please!"

"You look fine. It's becoming. Don't worry! Come in," she called. "Just walk in, Frank and Myra."

The sound of the door opening. "We're in." That was Frank.

"Straight ahead," Beth called, going to Louise's door.

Louise sat up straight. How strange that her heart was rocking inside her like a sign in a high wind. She thought she felt it banging against her ribs.

"Louise, dear!" Myra Weiss, bending over her, kissing her cheek. She was all angles and bones, very plain until she smiled. Her smile brought Louise a gust of hope that sent her heart rocking again. Myra's smile was generous, truthful.

"Myra, Mrs. Weiss—" Louise held onto the offered hand. She spoke rapidly, in a low voice. "What did Ma tell you about me?"

Myra extracted her hand, turned to Frank, saying, "Here, Frank, come over here and say hello to this girl."

"Well, well, long time—how are you, Louise?" He extended his hand, as if to shake hers, a look of confusion and distress passed over his face, and instead he bent toward her and kissed the air near her cheek.

They chatted, somehow. Myra talked about swimming, wasn't the heat beastly, their sons were going to camp next week, and what shows did Louise like to watch on TV?

Frank said he hoped Louise would work in his office again next summer. When Louise didn't answer, Myra said quickly that Louise was too old to be an errand girl, and anyway, she was bright and should go to college. The lies and smiles spun around her, sticky, trembling, sinister. Myra was restless, walked around the room, looked at everything on the bureau, straightened a picture on the wall, never settled down once. Frank rocked back and forth on small feet encased in soft black leather boots. He wore a white short-sleeved shirt, a silky black tie. Myra wore a sleeveless yellow, daisy-printed dress.

Louise smiled and smiled. How nice of them to come see her. Yes, yes, she loved visitors. Well, no, she didn't get that many; in fact, very often, most often, none at all. No, it seemed her friends were very busy. Sometimes, yes, the days were long when you had to spend them in bed. Oh, yes, she did sleep a bit, quite a bit. Yes. Yes.

At last Myra looked at the tiny gold watch on her wrist. They bent over her again, murmuring good-byes, take care, you'll be up and around in no time; at the door they lingered, looking back at her, then seemed to give, in unison, an extraordinary sigh of relief. "Well, good-bye. Good-bye! We'll drop in again." Then they were gone.

Louise lay back, exhausted, depleted. The past was a dream, the present a lie, the future, emptiness. If only she believed in God. Could she wind belief around her heart like a bandage, take it like a pill, inject it like a drug? If God was there (she imagined Him in hospital green, stethoscope dangling on his chest, reassuring smile showing beneath professionally blank eyes; God, Super Doc) He would X-ray her bones and find the marrow dissolving; X-ray her heart and find despair.

She dozed off, moaned, slept fitfully. When she woke, her mother was sitting on the side of her bed, a mustache of sweat over her upper lip. "It must have been a hundred degrees in the shop today," Ma said. "Was it awful here?" Her strong bare arms were moist.

"Ma, I was just dreaming about ocean water," Louise said. "A dream about being on the ocean. Remember when you took me and Beth to Atlantic City? And I went down in the glass bell under the water? The Wonderful World of Under Water, I think they called it. Remember?" Louise laughed. "Beth was too scared, so you had to stay on the boardwalk with her. And nobody else was going down that time. So it was just me and the man who ran it, and as we're descending, I kept saying, 'Well, where's the fish? Where's the Wonderful World of Under Water? I don't see anything!'"

Her mother started laughing, rocking back and forth, her arms around herself. "And you didn't know that everything you said was booming right up into the air through a mike, or something of the sort, booming right into the air where everyone could hear. 'Where's the fish?' you kept saying. 'This is a cheat, I want to see fish!'"

"There were no fish," Louise said. "No fish at all. They'd gotten smart, they weren't going to live around a dumb diving bell that messed up their lives."

Ma laughed softly. "That poor man. You must have ruined his business for the day."

"Ma, I'd like to go to the ocean again." As she said it, Louise was overcome with longing for the sea, for water blue as a child's crayon drawing: diving into the blue water, swimming naked among the silvery flash of fish, bare arms, two strong healthy legs, just she and the fish in the ocean.

"The ocean? You mean a cruise, honey?" Ma bent toward Louise, spreading out her hands. There was grime under her nails from the shop. "We'll do that, you'll be well by then. Next summer, we'll go on a cruise. I'll start saving up for it, beginning this week." She began to plan how much money she would save each week, what clothes they would take, how long they could spend.

"I'll save up my sick days, and we'll add that to my vacation time. Oh, we'll have a wonderful time, like the old days."

"Oh, Ma." Louise was sweating. "We'll never go."

"What?" Her mother, yanked from the dream, appeared dazed.

Louise turned her head, staring at the window, seeing dim Miss Moonface swimming in the glass. She tore the kerchief off her head, crumpling the silk in her hand.

"What is it?" Ma said, leaning forward, alert at once. "Are you in pain? Lou."

"No. Not pain. Not that way. Ma—" The day had been lie on lie on lie. The weight of the lies bore down on her. She was breaking under them. The lies were *killing* her. She couldn't keep hope away. She wasn't strong enough by herself. The hope that the lies they told her were true, that she would be healthy again, that she would be nineteen next year, that she would make love and go to the ocean and learn to dance on one leg, that she would get a job and read books and eat chili and travel to sunny California. "Tell me the truth," she groaned.

"The truth?" Ma's lips trembled. Her hand was on Louise's arm, pressing, pressing, her eyes were wet, begging. *Don't make me say it.*

"Ma—oh, God, Ma, I'm going to die, aren't I?"

"What! Lou—no, who said it? Who's upsetting you? Was it Frank Weiss?"

"Ma. Tell me. Say it. Do it for me, Ma," Louise begged. "I need you to say it! 'Louise, you're dying.'"

172

"No, no." Her mother wept helplessly. "No." Her cries rose shrilly. "No, no, no, no." She bent her head.

Louise was crying, too, rough gasps mingling with her mother's cries. "Ma, Ma," she wept, reaching out. They held each other, their tears, held back so long, telling the truth better than words. In a month she would be dead. Or it might be six weeks. Or two weeks. But soon.

"What's this? What are we doing?" her mother said, raising her head, wiping roughly at her cheeks. "Are we crazy—all these tears! We should be smiling—" She faltered, her eyes overflowing again.

"*Ma*, don't!" Louise held her mother's hand tightly. "I know. Ma, I want us to be like before. You, me, Bethie. No lies. No more. There isn't time."

Her mother slowly nodded her head. "I'll get supper now," she said. She smoothed the sheets over Louise. "I saw the prettiest linen in the store. Little bunches of flowers. Would you like that?"

"Yes," Louise said. From now on, forever, there would be only this bed, this room, this bit of sky. Beth, her mother.

From the kitchen she heard the comfortable clatter of dishes. Her throat still ached from the tears, but she felt peaceful. She ran her hand over the wrinkled sheet. For the night, Beth would give her clean fresh sheets smelling of the iron. She heard kids shouting in the alley between the two houses and looked out the window. There was the ordinary house she had seen from this same window every day of her life. But now she saw it with extraordinary clarity—the peeling chips of gray paint, the rough spots on the boards, the long rusty discolored line that ran beneath the drain. Her heart beat roughly. How good everything was.

In the little view of sky above roof, the layer of gray cloud lifted for the first time in a week, and a piece of blue sky appeared. Louise rolled over and pressed her face against the window, staring hungrily at the patch of sky, blue as the sea, clear, pure and perfect, coming to her like a gift.

Zelzah: A Tale from Long Ago

Her name was Zelzah. It meant Shade-in-the-Heat. She was the second oldest of five daughters. Before her came Ruth; after her, Shulamith, Anna, and Sarah. Zelzah, quiet, often wondered about the names her mother had given her and her sisters. Anna, for instance, whose name meant "grace," was clumsy, with one leg shorter than the other. "Cripple, cripple, drown and dripple," other children chanted at her as she limped and hopped in the dusty street outside their house. As for Shulamith, it seemed sometimes that she lived only to do everything possible to disprove the meaning of her name, which was "peacefulness."

Shulamith went into a rage at the smallest detail. She insisted on fairness: the potato kugel must be cut into five equal portions for the sisters; a hair ribbon for Sarah must be shared with Anna; a letter from Aunt Hannah in America must be read aloud to everyone, or

175

no one could hear it. "I insist," Shulamith cried. "I insist on fairness!"

The five sisters slept together in a large double bed. Although Ruth (friendship), who was wrong in the head, was the oldest, Shulamith dictated where each sister should sleep, and who would share what quilts. Anna and Sarah, the youngest, slept across the bottom of the bed, head to toe, reversing sides every night so that neither got poked too often by their elder sisters' feet. Zelzah slept sandwiched between Ruth and Shulamith. All night, Ruth, who never said much during the day, only smiled at everyone and everything, groaned and muttered in her sleep, while Shulamith flung her arms around and turned a dozen times from side to side. Between these two, and with the little girls defenseless at her feet, Zelzah learned to sleep without moving, lying still on her back, her hands crossed over her belly.

Still, she was only human and there were occasions when her leg or her arm slipped over the invisible boundary into Shulamith's territory. At once, Shulamith screamed with fury. "Off my side, off, off!"

"Shulamith, Shulamith, peace, peace," Zelzah's mother would say in despairing tones. The mother was a small woman: small-boned, small hands, small feet; she had once been a beauty. After five miscarriages and five live births, her beauty had faded: she had the worn, soft look of a piece of good linen that has been washed innumerable times. She had lived all her life in poverty and was an incurable optimist. Although her own name, Adah, meant ornament, and her whole life had been nothing but toil, she had still given each of her daughters a name she believed would help write her future.

"You are meant to be a comfort to those around you," she told Zelzah. "To your family now, to your husband and children someday. How wonderful it is to get out of the heat of summer into the shade! Just so, will your husband and children come to you for relief from strife and difficulties."

Zelzah loved this tiny mother who insisted against all evidence that names were destiny, and she tried very hard to live up to her name. She wanted to be a cool refreshing person, but summer or winter, her head sweated like a pig, her hands and feet were always red and burning, and in moments of stress she would be struck dumb. Thus, when Shulamith screamed at her in bed, "Off my side! Off, off, off!" Zelzah was helpless to calm her sister.

The bed the girls slept in stood in a corner of the one large whitewashed room that was their house. Besides the bed with its scrolled wooden headboard, the room contained a high dish cupboard, two wooden wardrobes, a scrubbed wooden table and chairs, several metal trunks with rounded tops and leather straps, a stove, and their parents' bed.

Each one of the girls had been born in that bed, each one had slept there for three or four years with her parents before moving into the bed with her sisters, to make room for the new baby.

Their father, Jacob, worked on leather; he was a tanner. He dragged himself home each night smelling horribly. His hands were permanently stained the color of old boots. Sometimes their mother wanted to sleep with the girls, but where could they find room for another body? They lived in Poland, they were Jewish, and all this was a good many years ago.

Of course they were poor. All the Jews in the little village of Premzl were poor. In Warsaw, they heard, there were wealthy Jews, Jews with servants, even, but here in Premzl goats were tethered by the houses, and chickens pecked in the streets.

Stories of America, the golden land, whistled between the houses like the wind. At night, Zelzah's parents whispered in their bed. Zelzah's mother sewed a pocket into the bottom of her mattress, and there, whenever she could, she put aside a bit of money. In the winter on market days she rose before dawn to bake rolls. She wrapped them in napkins, carried them to the market-place, and sold them, singing, "Hot rolls, hot hot hot, hot rolls." Under her skirt she kept a hot brick to warm her chilled feet and legs.

The girls, too, did whatever they could. Anna, the cripple, ran errands for the neighbors, her shoulders listing, accepting the coins she was given with a sullen smile. Ruth would do whatever task she was set to in the house. If no one told her to sweep the floor, or stir the washing in the tub on the stove, she would pick up a stick, a bug, a crushed leaf, and bringing it close to her eyes, stare at it for hours. Shulamith and Zelzah did a bit of everything. Only Sarah, the youngest ("princess"), was petted and allowed to play all day.

Zelzah: A Tale from Long Ago

At the age of nine, Zelzah went to work on the farm of an elderly Polish couple. The woman's fingers were bent like claws and she could no longer feed the chickens, do her housework, baking, and all the other things that had to be done on a farm. Zelzah took over these tasks. It was hard work, but she was well fed, and was often outdoors. She worked for the couple for six years, uncomplaining, walking three miles each way every day. Her hands were coarse and red. Her body became sturdy, and her arms were strong.

Her parents began to speak of her future. They wanted a good husband for their Zelzah. They discussed this boy, that boy, another one. Ruth, though older, would, of course, stay home with them. Zelzah would be the first of the sisters to marry. Zelzah listened, sometimes smiling, cracking her reddened knuckles, saying little. Then, on the farm, standing outside the cow's stall, for instance, her feet planted squarely in the mucky yard, holding a bucket of fresh warm milk, the flies thick on the rim, some already drowned in the milk, she would lift her face and squint into the distance. Strange thoughts went through her mind. A wind might be blowing gently. Or the sun shining. Goldfinches dipped across the fields. Life seemed wonderful, although she didn't know why and would never have said it aloud. The thought of marriage made her sigh over and over.

"I want to get married," Shulamith whispered fiercely into Zelzah's ear at night. "Why did Mama have you before me? I want to have my own bed and sleep in it with a man!"

Zelzah snorted behind her hand. Shulamith tickled her suddenly, and Zelzah thrashed around, shrieking with laughter.

Later that summer, a letter from Aunt Hannah came from America, from a town named Stratton in a place called Vermont. Aunt Hannah had four sons, "all good, kind boys, and smart, too," she wrote. One was already married to an American girl. One was still young. Two sons, Jake and Ephraim, needed wives. Aunt Hannah thought Zelzah, now fifteen, would make a good wife for her son Jake. She would pay half Zelzah's boat fare.

Zelzah's mother counted her little hoard of money. There was enough for half a boat fare plus a little extra to give Zelzah wrapped in a handkerchief which was then tucked carefully into the wicker case with leather straps that held her clothing.

Cold winds blew in the village when Zelzah left. The boat would be cold. She wore a gray wool blouse, a long black worsted skirt, a heavy coat that had been her father's and that smelled like a tannery, a scarf on her head and a wool shawl over her shoulders. The shawl, gray, with black fringe, was her mother's. On the boat, Zelzah wept into the fringe. She was not seasick, she endured without complaint the crowding, the stifling odors, the groans, noises, and cries of the hundreds of people with whom she was packed into steerage; once every day she ate bread and a bit of hard dry cheese with good appetite. Yet, for the forty-two days of the voyage, tears poured steadily from her eyes.

Aunt Hannah met her at the dock in New York City.

Thank God, Aunt Hannah looked like Zelzah's mother, her very own sister! How else would Zelzah have known that this was, indeed, her aunt, and not just one of the hundreds of women milling around?

Aunt Hannah hugged Zelzah. She was small, like Zelzah's mother, with the same bright black eyes, but with prematurely white hair. And her cheeks, unlike her sister's, were bright, blooming. She pinched Zelzah's cheek and said in Yiddish, "You're a fine, strong-looking girl. Tell me how my sister is, tell me everything!"

"Yes, they're fine, all fine," Zelzah said, looking around. The noise made her ears ache. She longed to close her eyes against the swarms of people, carts, horses, buildings, signs, wagons, dogs, and God knew what else! It had really happened, then! She had left home, crossed the ocean, come to America. Remembering the tears she had wept on the voyage, her eyes ached as if to shed more tears. She stuffed the fringes of her shawl into her mouth and followed Aunt Hannah.

They took a train to Vermont, and from the station walked two miles to the village. It was night. There was snow everywhere in great dazzling white drifts. The stars were icy in the dark sky. Zelzah walked beside Aunt Hannah, her breath blowing out before her in a white cloud. Her wicker case bumped against her leg, the snow crunched beneath her feet. Aunt Hannah told her about the small grocery store she and Uncle Morris owned in Stratton. In Zelzah's honor, Aunt Hannah said, the store was closed early.

They came to a wooden building, two stories high.

Aunt Hannah led the way up a dim, narrow flight of stairs. "Here we are, dear child!"

Zelzah was trembling. Her legs felt weak. There was a blur of male faces and voices. Uncle Morris, a short sweaty man with tight gray curls, embraced her, his long soft mustache brushing her face. His eyes were kind. Her cousins were introduced, one, two, three, Jake, Ephraim, Sammy. Michel, the oldest, was married and had gone west with his bride. All this Zelzah heard as if from a distance. Her stomach rocked as if now, off the boat, she was for the first time, seasick.

"Sit down, sit down." Uncle Morris pushed her into a large overstuffed chair. "Hannah, bring some wine. Ephraim, here, take your cousin's case." But Zelzah wouldn't release her grip on the wicker case.

The room she was in was crowded with furniture; couches, a dark oak sideboard on top of which trays, glasses, bottles, and framed pictures bumped against one another, many little tables with kerosene lamps, ashtrays, a piano, and a large gate-leg table overflowing with books and papers. Small woven rugs were scattered around on the carpeted floor, and thick red velvet curtains, their tassels sweeping the floor, covered the windows. Zelzah's head spun, her ears were burning, her head sweating. With moist burning hands, she clutched the wicker case, nodding and bobbing her head.

Downstairs, behind the store, there was still another room; here, Aunt Hannah had made a place for Zelzah. She had laid a colorful little rag rug on the wooden floor, and the rocking chair had a bright red cushion. A calendar hung on a nail, showing a picture of a deer fleeing into snow-covered woods. The date of Zelzah's arrival was circled. There was a bed, and a marble-topped bureau with three drawers and a special place for the white chamber pot that had a bunch of daisies painted on the side.

"You're so kind, so very kind, too kind," Zelzah said. It was very cold, the windows were iced with frost flowers. Zelzah stared shyly at the iron cot with its single mattress covered by a gray wool blanket. Imagine. A bed just for her.

After Aunt Hannah left, Zelzah sat on the edge of the bed, staring down at her heavy black shoes. How handsome Cousin Ephraim was! There was something dashing and bold about him, about his bold black eyes, and thick black mustache. His eyes had danced over her as he greeted her in English. When she stammered something in Yiddish, he had laughed and pinched her cheek as if she were so much younger than he. Then he had turned to his mother and said something quickly, again in English, which had made Aunt Hannah laugh and swat his hands lightly. Zelzah was glad he was not the one Aunt Hannah wanted her for.

As for Jake, she had only peeked at him, keeping her scarf over her head and drawn almost down to her eyes, out of fear and shyness. "How do you do, dear cousin, are you tired from the trip?" he had said. Such kind words. Jake wasn't handsome like Ephraim, but—beautiful! She had never seen a man so beautiful. His eyes were as blue as the sky over the Polish farm on a summer day, his nose was long and fine, his mouth full, soft, gentle. He wore soft leather boots, and the hand that pressed hers in greeting was dry and cool. "Ah," she sighed, astonished by his beauty.

Each morning of her new life, Zelzah woke before dawn, as she always had, dressed hurriedly in the frigid room, used the outside "facilities," and joined the family for breakfast. Sammy went each day to school, Ephraim to work in an office, Jake to work in the paper mill, while Zelzah joined Uncle Morris and Aunt Hannah in the store. On the first day, speaking kindly but firmly, Aunt Hannah said, "Now, Zelzah, no more Yiddish. You must learn to speak like an American."

Through the winter and into the spring, she worked in the store. At first she hardly dared speak, but little by little she learned American phrases, American money, and American behavior. She gave up wearing her shawl in public, and did her best not to embarrass the family.

At night, though, she still slept with the shawl next to her face and often wept into its fringes. She thought of her sisters, and especially of Shulamith. How quiet these sons of Aunt Hannah were! She couldn't get accustomed to sleeping alone in a bed, to being all alone through the night in a room with not another soul in it.

Often she lay awake for hours, staring into the dark, straining to hear—something. A sigh, a groan, a cough, the whispers of her parents as they lay together. Outside, dogs barked. Or an owl hooted. Far away, a horse might whinny. The night was no darker than all the other nights of her life had been, but she lay awake, her heart swollen with terror and loneliness.

Yet everyone was kind to her. Uncle Morris gave her chocolates and patted her head reassuringly when she made mistakes. Ephraim teased that he was getting tired of these American girls who couldn't stay away from him, and said, laughingly, "Watch out, brother Jake!" Aunt Hannah was pleased with every American word Zelzah learned and praised the immaculate way she kept her room and her person.

Her young cousin, Sammy, sometimes showed her his schoolbooks, pointing out a word here and there. As for Jake, he spoke to her gravely, asking her questions about her sisters, the work she had done on the farm, the village where she had lived. He listened to everything she said, his eyes melancholy. She wondered what made him sad. When she lapsed into Yiddish, he shook his head reproachfully. "Speak English, Zelzah. Yiddish is for greenies." He spent most of his time reading books. Zelzah had never read a whole book. In the summer, they were to be married.

The weather was still cold, although winter had re-treated, when Jake came to Zelzah's room one night. He got into her bed. His bony legs and feet were icy. Zelzah held him close, warming him. He came to her bed one or two nights every week. After his visits, Zelzah always slept more soundly. She thought Jake's eyes were not so sad anymore. As he lay in her arms, she whispered to him in Yiddish, "I would like a cat when we have our

185

own home." She had never asked anyone for anything; it struck her that she was becoming brave, even American. She rubbed her hands in Jake's hair. He smelled good, like fresh-baked bread. He was always cold, and she was always warm, burning, her head steaming: She thought of her name, Shade-in-the-Heat; was not warmth in winter just as good?

In spring, Ephraim, who had many girlfriends, brought home a new girl to meet his mother. Her name was Grace. She was a college student and spoke quickly, laughing often. "How do you do!" she said to Zelzah, holding out her hand and then shaking Zelzah's hand forcefully. She was a tall girl with long hands and feet. "So you're reading Dickens," she said to Jake. "He's out of fashion, but I think he's wonderful, don't you?"

The next time Grace came to the house, she and Jake and Ephraim all went out for a walk in the fresh evening. Zelzah was glad they didn't ask her. She felt shy and ignorant around Grace. Soon, Grace began to drop in on her own, often when Ephraim wasn't around. She and Jake argued furiously about books and politics. Then, for a while, she stopped coming to the house. And Jake stopped coming to Zelzah's room at night.

Well, well, Zelzah said to herself several months later, it's not surprising. No, not surprising. She seemed to be quite calm. She listened calmly as Aunt Hannah, weeping and hugging her, said that Grace was pregnant, that in fact Grace and Jake had been secretly married for some time.

They were in Zelzah's little room behind the store,

sitting on the iron cot with its neatly laid blanket. "Oh, what a disgrace, I'm so ashamed," Aunt Hannah said, looking at Zelzah with reddened eyes. She seized Zelzah's hands. "And I promised my sister—" Fresh tears threatened. She drew Zelzah's hands to her heart. "Dear child! Do you want to stay on? You're always welcome. But they are going to live here. Grace and Jake. Until the baby is born, at least. Oh, what will you do now?"

"I will think of something," Zelzah said, in Yiddish. She felt a little cold and hunched her shoulders, drawing her mother's shawl closer around herself.

It was now fall again, nearly a year since Zelzah had come to America. Uncle Morris and Aunt Hannah went with her to the train station. She carried her wicker case and a bag of fruit and sandwiches Aunt Hannah had made for her. "You can always come back," Aunt Hannah said. "If you need us, we're here, right here!"

Uncle Morris pressed a chunk of white chocolate, and then a five-dollar bill into her hands. Zelzah boarded the train, took a seat and put her wicker case at her feet. Her hands were sticky with chocolate. She put the chocolate down on the seat, tucked the money into the little leather purse Aunt Hannah had given her, and wiped her hands on her handkerchief. The train jerked and puffed. She looked out the cinder-specked window. Aunt Hannah and Uncle Morris were waving, moving alongside the train as it slowly left the station.

"Good-bye, good-bye," Zelzah said. Her eyes were moist, but suddenly she wanted to laugh. A wind seemed to blow through her, and she recalled the blue Polish sky and goldfinches bobbing over the fields. She drew the handkerchief to her mouth so that Aunt Hannah and Uncle Morris wouldn't see her laughing. The train picked up speed.

In New York City she found her way to a family whom Aunt Hannah had recommended. Here she was given a bed and meals for a small sum. She found work almost at once in a dress factory situated in a loft. All winter she sat at a sewing machine for nine hours a day, six days a week. She made $11 a week. She was nearly seventeen years old.

Work in the factory was hard; the loft was boiling in the summer, freezing in the winter. But Zelzah was strong. Two nights a week she went to school to learn to read and write English. Every month she sent money to her family; Shulamith was planning to come to America to join Zelzah.

In spring Zelzah heard from Aunt Hannah that Grace had died in childbirth. She remembered Grace saying, "I think Dickens is wonderful!" She sat up for many hours that night thinking about her life, thinking of Jake with his cold feet and bony legs. Now he had an infant girl, but no wife to care for the child or him. Zelzah had begun to see that there were things she might like to do in the world. She had left her village in Poland, traveled across Europe, then the Atlantic Ocean. She had gone from New York to Vermont, and back to New York. Now she knew there were other places to go, and she thought that she would no longer be afraid to go to them. Pennsylvania! Wisconsin! North Carolina!

South Dakota! The names rang like bells in her head. She was reading the newspapers now, and sometimes a book. She had bought herself a few new clothes, a coat, shoes, a muff for her hands on bitter mornings.

She thought of all this, of the money she sent home, of the hope of Shulamith joining her. And then of her mother telling her the meaning of her name, the meaning of her life.

After this, she wrote a letter in English, being careful to spell each word properly. "My Dear Cousin Jake, I have heard recently of your Tragic News. I send you my Heartfelt Sympathy. There are tears in my Heart, for you. I want to say something in Plain Words. Would you need me now to be your wife? If that is the Truth, I will be happy to oblige." (She crossed out "to oblige.") "Kiss the dear little baby Girl for me. Zelzah."

And Jake answered, "Zelzah, dear cousin, my heart is too full of grief to consider this matter now. My mother takes care of the child, and I am going to Michigan to see if I can obtain the college education I so deeply desire, and which my beloved wife (whom I will mourn forever) believed I ought to have. Your cousin, in friendship, Jake Neuborg."

Reading Jake's letter, again that impulse to laugh overcame Zelzah. Although there was no one to see her, she stuffed her fingers into her mouth, stifling the laughter. She didn't understand herself. Was this a laughing matter!

Several years passed. At last Shulamith came to America. She wore high black boots and looked around her, scowling ferociously. "This noise, this noise!" She clapped her hands to her ears.

"You'll get used to it," Zelzah said, calmly. Passing through the throngs of people, gripping her sister firmly by the elbow, Zelzah caught sight of herself in a store window. She had changed. It was the first thing Shulamith had said. "Zelzah, is it you?" She had cut her hair; then, working and studying without much rest, eating less so she could send money home—these things had honed her down. She no longer had plump, bright-red cheeks. She was surprised, even a little alarmed to see herself; then she smiled.

Shulamith went to work in the same dress factory as Zelzah, but at once she hated it. She raged against it every day. "I'm getting out of here, I won't go on for years like you, Zelzah. Don't you ever get angry? Look at you, smiling, and you were jilted by our cousin. If a man ever did that to me!"

At night, she shoved Zelzah in the bed they shared. "Move! Move! You're on my side." Often, Zelzah got out of bed and read into the middle of the night, the fringed shawl over her shoulders.

In the morning, Shulamith was always up first. She prepared breakfast for the two of them. Sometimes she sang, but when the factory came into sight, she broke off, scowling, and raised her fist to the ugly building. She began night school also, but was not in the same class as Zelzah.

Zelzah was now hoping to get a high school diploma. She was studying mathematics, history, and geography.

When she and Shulamith walked to school, they linked arms, and Shulamith spoke of their parents and sisters, answering Zelzah's questions.

On warm Sundays, they often took the trolley to Brooklyn to walk in the woods, picking mushrooms or bunches of soft floppy little violets. One day, coming upon a farm, they sat on a bench and were given mugs of thick yellow milk.

"I used to milk cows," Zelzah said.

"You!" The farm woman smiled disbelievingly. "You!"

Linking hands, suddenly, like two children, Zelzah and Shulamith danced around, shouting with laughter. And the farm woman laughed, too, seeing that she was right and Zelzah, the young lady from the city, had only been teasing.

On one of these Sunday expeditions, Shulamith met a "landsman," a red-haired young man from a village near Premzl. The first time he came to visit them, Shulamith left the room, leaving Aaron and Zelzah together.

"Don't do that again," Zelzah said that night when she and Shulamith were alone, getting ready for bed. Shulamith, frowning, brushed her hair over her face.

"And why not? He can come to see you, as well as me!"

"Listen, my dear child," Zelzah said, as if she were years older than Shulamith, rather than only ten months. "I have no interest in the young man."

"But you're older," Shulamith said, brushing her hair furiously. "It's only fair! I want you to be happy!"

"Peace, Shulamith, peace," Zelzah said, just as their mother had done so many years ago.

Aaron was a locksmith; a good trade. Shulamith's rages left him undismayed; he had an even temperament and thought her quite wonderful. A year after they met, they were married. Shulamith insisted that the wedding pictures include Zelzah.

As the three of them stood outside Temple Beth Israel with their arms around each other, free hands holding down their hats against the warm gusts of May wind, Zelzah thought of the last letter she had received from her mother. "I long to see my dear Zelzah, my dear Shade-in-the-Heat. Send me good news soon! If I cannot see you, then the news of your happiness will satisfy me." Anna had been married the previous spring; Sarah was engaged. Only Ruth, who still stared for hours with dreamy satisfaction at a stick of wood (or so Shulamith had told her), and Zelzah were still unmarried.

The next year when Shulamith had her first child, Zelzah received her high school diploma. She left the factory and went to work in an office. Not more money, but far less strenuous work. Her eyes had been going bad in the factory; now she had to wear glasses for reading and close work. "So?" Shulamith said, when Zelzah visited to give her the good news of her new job. "Will you settle down now?"

Zelzah started college classes at night. For eleven years she went to college. For eleven years, each time she had an exam, she found it impossible to sleep and sat up all night with the gray fringed shawl over her shoulders, feverishly muttering dates, names, places, and formulas to herself. Only once did she fail an exam, in physics; that was the year when two days before the exam Shulamith had her third child and nearly died.

After she received her bachelor's degree, Zelzah was offered a job teaching third grade in a medium-sized city in upstate New York. There she rented a three-room apartment in a private home. The house was painted a fresh yellow on the outside, and had a large porch running around three sides. Zelzah had her own entrance, a tiny but efficient kitchen, and windows looking out on the back and side yards where the landlady, Mrs. Zimmerman, kept flowers and bushes blooming seven months of the year.

Every summer Zelzah visited Shulamith, Aaron, and their six children in the bungalow they rented in the Catskill Mountains. She stayed with them for a week or ten days, playing with the children, and talking to Shulamith for hours on end. She adored her nieces and nephews; she thought them all clever and beautiful, and she was always glad to leave the excitement and untidiness of their lives.

Thus, Zelzah's life. Her cats, interesting creatures. Her windows full of plants. A month of travel in the summer. Shulamith, Aaron, and the children. (She kept all their letters and notes in a little square metal candy box with blue flowers painted all over it.) And her third-grade students; often they returned years later to visit her, to tell her what they were doing, and how well they were doing it. She remembered all their names.

The winter of her fortieth birthday, Zelzah received a letter from Shulamith. "You could still get married," she wrote. "You are better-looking now than when you were younger. Come to visit us over the winter holidays, I want you to meet a friend. He was widowed six months ago. A lovely man! I want you to be happy!"

But Zelzah was involved with a pageant her third-grade children were writing and producing. There would be rehearsals over the vacation. The pageant was about the spirit of America and how the children's parents had come from so many different lands. Really, the children had done a lovely job! She wrote Shulamith her regrets. "Perhaps another time, I'll be able to come in the winter."

A few months later, she woke up one morning and thought how strange life was. It was 6 A.M. She had never shaken the habit of rising early. Zelzah had been dreaming about her sisters. She seemed to hear Shulamith shouting, "Move! It isn't fair!" She thought of the Polish farm, the dirty cows, herself a child dreaming with a bucket of warm milk in each hand. She thought of Jake pressing his cold body against hers. And of frost flowers on the window. Of the chocolates Uncle Morris had given her, and of drinking thick yellow milk in a farmyard. She thought of blue-covered examination books, the angry red faces of each one of Shulamith's babies, and then of the pink dress she had bought herself for spring.

A cat jumped on her stomach and began cleaning her paws. Zelzah pushed the cat to one side and, with her hands behind her head, did twenty sit-ups. She got out of bed and put her mother's shawl around her shoulders.

She held the shawl to her face for a moment, then washed in cold water. Mother and father, both, were long dead. She made herself coffee, ate an orange and buttered toast. She thought of the day ahead of her, of the children she would teach. She set down her coffee cup and hastened to get dressed. She was humming under her breath, her mind was filled with details of the day ahead of her. Was she happy? Who could say? Zelzah, herself, never thought in such terms. What was happiness? Did anyone know?

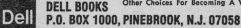